RACE AGAINST TIME

Christy Barritt

Love Inspired

Recycling programs for this product may not exist in your area.

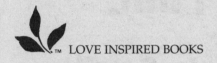 LOVE INSPIRED BOOKS

ISBN-13: 978-0-373-67507-4

RACE AGAINST TIME

www.LoveInspiredBooks.com

Printed in U.S.A.

"I'm going to keep an eye on you, Madison. Make sure you stay safe," Brody said. "It's going to be okay."

"I wish I felt so certain." What about Lincoln? What if the man who attacked her came back and tried to harm her son? She couldn't bear the thought of it. Perhaps she should simply take Lincoln and go somewhere, anywhere.

"We'll catch him, Madison." Brody's voice sounded confident, reassuring. It was as if he could read her mind.

Just then, they pulled up to her house.

With each step she took toward her back door, nausea rumbled in her gut. Could she face this nightmare again? She swallowed as they stepped inside, trying to stay strong. Brody led her to the foyer.

"I've got you," he said, a reassuring hand on her arm.

Books by Christy Barritt

Love Inspired Suspense

Keeping Guard
The Last Target
Race Against Time

CHRISTY BARRITT

loves stories and has been writing them for as long as she can remember. She gets her best ideas when she's supposed to be paying attention to something else—like in a workshop or while driving down the road.

The second book in her Squeaky Clean Mystery series, *Suspicious Minds,* won the inspiration category of the 2009 Daphne du Maurier Award for Excellence in Suspense and Mystery. She's also the co-author of *Changed: True Stories of Finding God in Christian Music.*

When she's not working on books, Christy writes articles for various publications. She's also a weekly feature writer for the *Virginian-Pilot* newspaper, the worship leader at her church and a frequent speaker at various writers groups, women's luncheons and church events.

She's married to Scott, a teacher and funny man extraordinaire. They have two sons, two dogs and a houseplant named Martha.

To learn more about her, visit her website, www.christybarritt.com.

My God is my rock, in whom I take refuge,
my shield and the horn of my salvation.
He is my stronghold, my refuge and my savior—
from violent men You save me.
—2 *Samuel* 22:3

This book is dedicated to my mom, Louise Mohorn,
a beautiful soul inside and out,
and someone I aspire to be like. I love you!

ONE

As soon as Madison Jacobs stepped into her house, the sound of ticking crept from an unknown crevice and reverberated in her ears. She froze at the front door, car keys still in hand, and listened. She usually came home to the solitude of a quiet house.

So what in the world was that noise?

She'd only been gone twenty minutes—long enough to drop her son off at preschool and return home. Each tick tightened her nerves, winding them with more tension than a spring.

Lincoln must have left the timer going on one of his toys, she realized. Didn't that windup dragon make a similar sound? Yes, it did.

Madison let out an airy laugh, shook her head and closed the door, shutting out the bright rays of sunshine from outside. Of course, one of her son's toys was to blame. What else did she think it was? A bomb? She chastised herself again for her out-of-control imagination.

Out of habit she clicked the lock on the front door into place. Being a single mom for the past three years, she tried to err on the side of caution. After depositing her purse and keys on the marble-topped table in the foyer, she glanced at her watch and saw she only had one hour before she had to meet with her next client. She had to get showered and changed out of her yoga pants and T-shirt—and fast.

As she started down the hallway toward the bedroom in her ranch house, the ticking intensified. She paused at the bathroom door. Was that where the sound came from? Reaching inside the bathroom, she flipped on the lights. Her blue-and-yellow lighthouse-themed room came into view. On the bathroom counter between the faucet and the soap dispenser sat her son's old-fashioned egg timer. Had Lincoln actually taken her advice to brush his teeth for two minutes this morning? Perhaps he'd accidentally set the clock for longer.

She picked the plastic device up, noting it was set to chime in twenty minutes, and twisted the handle until the bells jangled. Her nerves seemed to stretch tighter at the sound.

But if her son had set the timer before they'd left this morning, why hadn't she heard anything? She remembered their rushed departure. The TV had been on, Lincoln had been singing his favorite preschool song, and she had been frantically trying to urge him out the door.

Her schedule was tight today and she couldn't afford to even start it a minute late, knowing if she did her tardiness would have a domino effect and put her behind on all of her appointments.

She tossed the timer into a drawer that overflowed with hairbrushes and toy boats, and then hurried across the hall to the spare bedroom-turned-office. Finding her calendar, she checked her schedule one more time and reviewed her assignments for the day. Just seeing the jam-packed list made her feel weary. But she had to squeeze in as much work as possible. Making ends meet as a single parent was becoming harder and harder.

She closed the calendar and, wasting no more time, went into the master bathroom. After showering she towel dried her shoulder-length honey-blond hair and threw on some khakis and a button-up white top. Five minutes later she'd applied make up, grabbed her camera from her office and started down the hall. She had fifteen minutes to get to her appointment. Time would be tight, but she could do it.

She froze midway down the hall and placed a hand on her hip.

What was that sound?

She shook her head. It couldn't be…

Tick, tick, tick, tick, tick.

Fear pricked her skin.

The timer? She'd turned it off. Thrown it in the drawer.

Was she hearing things? The sound was subtle, subdued. Maybe the device had started again in the drawer? The thing was cheap, often turning off in the middle of one of Lincoln's time-out sessions. Had it turned on by itself now?

She sighed and stepped back into the hallway bathroom. Flipping on the light, she yanked the drawer open and found the timer exactly where she'd thrown it. She picked it up and shook her head. Cheap thing. It had been free, sent as a part of an advertising campaign for some new company in town. What was that slogan? Don't Let Time Run Out on Our Special? Clever.

Before she could twist the plastic white timer off, the bell jangled.

Madison jumped, dropping her camera bag onto the tiled bathroom floor. Papers detailing today's work scattered all over the room. Hand over her heart, she laughed at herself. Silly woman. Jumping at nothing.

She dropped the timer back into the drawer, shaking her head. Why was she so skittish? And over something so silly?

She caught a glance of herself in the mirror over the sink, noting the circles under her eyes.

She'd been working too much lately, worried too much about finances. She leaned toward her reflection and wiped a streak of mascara under her eye. As she turned to leave, something in the mirror caught her eye.

She glanced at the reflection of the shower curtain behind her.

Her heart froze.

A man stood there, a knife in his hand. Before she could scream, he grabbed her.

Brody Philips always considered sweat a good measure of hard work. If that was the case, then his jog this morning should earn him a vacation. He continued on his ten-mile run, nearly finished now. The hot and muggy day couldn't even be eased by the gentle breeze that floated from the Chesapeake Bay.

The part of the Bay he lived by wasn't the sandy beach area. Instead, marsh grasses jutted up and little streams filled with tadpoles and crabs meandered between the foliage. Herons and egrets made their homes in the sun-bleached wetland area. Finally the grasses subsided until the glorious blue of the bay shone in the distance.

His house—actually, his cousin's house that had been kindly loaned out to Brody for the next several months while his cousin was stationed with the army in the Middle East—stood in the distance. He passed the home of his one and only neighbor on the secluded street.

He'd met her once. Madison Jacobs. She'd come over that first week after he'd moved in to introduce herself. She seemed nice enough and certainly she was easy on the eyes. But Brody hadn't moved here to make friends, not even acquaintances, really. He'd moved here to get away from everything about his past in New York.

The secluded little Virginia town was the perfect spot for his self-imposed hiatus from his old life. He'd taken a job as a detective for the county's sheriff's department, one that was considerably slower paced than his former position in the Big Apple. Aside from his job, he avoided most of the townspeople when possible and whenever he needed a dose of anonymity, he visited the nearby city of Newport News or headed to Virginia Beach.

His neighbor had seemed to take the hint and hadn't bothered him since that first introduction when he'd moved in. The woman—pretty with her sun-kissed skin, natural blond hair, and sparkling blue eyes—would smile tightly and wave as she passed him in her SUV coming and going. The action wasn't overly exuberant, but appeared to be more of a forced courtesy.

Perhaps he should have been friendlier when she'd rung his doorbell, toddler and cookies in tow. He'd taken one look at her and known that getting to know her better would be way too tempting. Instead, he'd done the opposite and offered as little information about himself as possible before insisting he was in the middle of something so she'd go home. Her eyes had changed from friendly to perceptive and then annoyed as he'd closed the door. Good. It was better that way.

As his feet hit the dusty road, rocks crunching beneath him, a sharp, high-pitched sound split the air.

Brody slowed his pace and wiped the perspiration around his face with the bottom of his T-shirt. Was that a scream? Or was it the shrieking call of one of the marsh birds?

He glanced at Madison's house. Her car was in the driveway, but he didn't see her anywhere. She must be inside, either chasing her toddler or doing some work. He couldn't be positive, but his best guess was that the woman worked at home.

His jog slowed to a walk, and he kept his ear attuned for any more sounds. Nothing. He must have imagined the earlier noise.

He tried to be satisfied with that, but he wasn't convinced. He *was* a detective. His finely trained instincts told him to stay on guard.

Something crashed in the distance. The sound had definitely come from Madison's house. His muscles tensed. He should go back to his house, get his gun. But everything in him screamed to get to her house, that time couldn't be wasted.

He ran across crunchy grass toward his neighbor's brick ranch. His gaze scanned the house as he approached. Nothing appeared out of place. The closed shades made it impossible to see inside.

He crept onto the wooden porch, grabbing a baseball bat left on a rocking chair. Slowly he twisted the brass handle of the front door.

Locked.

Something else crashed inside. A woman cried out.

He pictured Madison's pretty face and imagined the horrors that might be going on inside. Adrenaline surged in him. He backed up and, on the count of three, charged forward. His shoulder impacted with the door. Wood split, cracked, then crashed.

The foyer stood before him. Dust and wood particles settled to the tile floor. Then an eerie quiet filled the space.

"Hello? Anyone home?" Brody stepped over the door, his ears attuned for any telltale signs. Bat in hand, he peered around the corner into the hallway.

A shadow passed by a door in the distance.

Sucking in a deep breath, he braced himself for whatever was to come.

Blurry. Fuzzy. Jumbled.

The drugs—whatever the masked man had injected into her—caused Madison's thoughts to swirl. *Fight it, Madison. Fight it.* She couldn't let herself fall into unconsciousness. The rope around her neck would choke her if she did. She had to resist the urge to close her eyes. Fight death. Fight for life.

Her head bobbed forward and the rope dug into her neck. She jerked back. Gulped in a breath.

Lord, give me strength.

But her limbs felt like gelatin. The stool she stood on wobbled. The man who wanted her dead would return and finish his cruel game.

A moan escaped her, the sound guttural, desperate.

Her head fell forward again. She gagged. Pulled her head back. Gasped for air.

Lincoln. She blinked, trying to find focus. She had to fight this for him. The boy couldn't lose two parents before he reached the age of five. Tears pricked her eyes as her son's sweet face flashed in her mind. She needed to be there for him, to comfort him when he got hurt, to tuck him into bed at night.

Her tears made breathing hard. She couldn't let herself fall into despair. She had to stay strong.

But how long could she stand here? How long before the drugs kicked in and knocked her out completely? Was there any hope of surviving?

Her eyes darted around the room. Where had the man gone? And had she heard a crash or imagined it? What was the madman planning next?

Her head dipped. Her airway constricted.

Not much longer.

She jerked her head back, fighting to stay lucid. But tiredness closed in on her.

A figure appeared in the doorway. Not again. What would her attacker do this time? She cried out, tried to back up. The rope tightened around her neck.

"It's just me." The man rushed toward her.

Madison blinked. Her neighbor? Or was this a hallucination? Maybe she'd already drifted into an unconscious state and the drugs were playing tricks on her mind.

"Madison." He muttered the word. His arms encircled her waist and raised her up. She gulped in breaths, thankful for relief.

But her relief was short-lived. Her head whirled. Blackness closed in on her.

"Don't fade now. I'm going to get you down. Do you hear me?"

She nodded, but it was already too late. Everything went dark.

TWO

The nightmare from Brody's past flooded his mind, making nausea roil in his stomach. Horrifying images and intense emotions flashed through him, each one feeling like a sock in the gut. He blanched before pushing the thoughts away. No time to dwell on that now. If he didn't act quickly a woman could die in his arms.

His gaze searched the room. He had to find something to cut his neighbor down from the ceiling. But if he released her to search for a knife, she'd choke.

His heart racing, he continued searching with his eyes, looking for something…anything.

Nothing. Just some clothes on the dresser. A hair brush. Shoes. Pillows. Typical bedroom items.

Think, Brody. Think.

His muscles strained. The woman was a deadweight in his arms. She'd lost consciousness and it was only a matter of time before she lost her life.

Adrenaline surged through him. Not again.

He looked at the ceiling fan that held the rope and made a split-second decision. Still holding Madison with one arm, he grabbed the fan's motor. Using all of his strength, he jerked down on the device.

The ceiling cracked.

He gripped the motor tighter and, yanking up his legs, let his weight do the rest of the job. The entire fan tumbled to the floor, himself and Madison with it. He didn't bother to brush off the plaster that covered them. Instead he grabbed the rope around his neighbor's neck. He pulled the noose until it widened enough to jerk it off. Then he went to work on the ties around her wrists.

She lay limp in his arms. He did a quick examination. Red, raw skin surrounded her neck. Torn shirt. Bleeding forehead. But she was breathing. Thank goodness she was breathing.

Any minute now an ambulance and the sheriff should be here. He'd grabbed a phone from a table in the foyer and hit 911 before proceeding down the hallway.

He gently shook the woman. "Madison? Madison? Can you hear me?"

She moaned.

What exactly had happened in here? Had

the woman—who had seemed mild mannered enough—flown into a rage before deciding to end her own life? Could that be what the sounds were that he'd heard? It was the only explanation that made sense.

Sirens sounded in the distance.

"Help's coming," he whispered, pushing the woman's hair back from her face. "Help is coming."

He only hoped they'd get here fast enough.

Brody paced the hospital hallway, waiting for the doctor to give him the go-ahead to speak with his neighbor about what had happened. The rubber soles of his athletic shoes squeaked against the shiny linoleum floor, the noise offset by the sound of machines beeping and nurses murmuring and a lunch cart rattling.

He couldn't get the image of Madison hanging by a rope attached to the ceiling fan out of his mind.

It reminded him so much of Lindsey...

He squeezed his eyes shut. He couldn't go there. He had to ignore the memories that slammed into his mind with enough force that an ache began to throb at the back of his head.

Instead, he replayed the events from today. What would drive a woman with a small son to try and commit suicide? He knew her husband had died in an auto accident a few years ago. His cousin had told him that much. Had Madison, who always seemed so pleasant and warm, decided she couldn't take it anymore? He would never have guessed her to be the type, but he'd also learned in his years as a detective that you never knew what went on behind closed doors. The most put-together person could in reality be a total mess, just be a master at disguising it.

Something nagged at Brody. Though it appeared his neighbor had tried to commit suicide, something felt wrong. He remembered the noise he'd heard as he jogged outside her home. It almost sounded as if she was being attacked. The noise must have been coming from Madison, though, because there was no evidence to suggest foul play.

"Detective Philips?" The nurse behind the counter called him. He could tell by her gaze that she found him attractive. He knew enough to be able to read that from her wide smile and doelike eyes.

He stepped forward. "Yes?"

She dangled the phone toward him. "The sheriff wants to speak to you."

He crossed the hall and took the phone, giving the nurse a brief smile. "Detective Philips here."

"Just wanted to let you know that we found a suicide note. I don't know what Madison did before hanging herself. The house is a wreck. But it's definitely an attempted suicide."

Brody wasn't sure why he felt disappointed. He'd wanted to believe his neighbor wasn't capable of wanting to end her own life. He didn't know her, but perhaps he'd made up his own version of what she'd be like. She seemed to have everything so together, to be such a loving mother. She wouldn't purposely leave her son an orphan...would she?

"Thanks for letting me know." He cleared his throat. "What did it say?"

"Basically that she loves her family, but she can't get over the heartache of losing her husband. Poor girl has had a bad run of luck since Reid died. I've known her since she was in diapers. I never thought I'd see this day. Never."

"No one ever does."

"Be kind to her, you hear? I'd be there myself, but I'm on my way to a drunk-driving accident. You tell her I'll be checking on her later."

"Of course." He handed the phone back to the nurse, careful not to smile back again and give the woman the wrong idea.

So, it had been a suicide attempt. He crossed his arms and leaned against the wall. He still wore his jogging clothes. He hadn't had time to go home and change. The sheriff had ordered that he go with the paramedics to the hospital and write up a report. For some strange reason, Brody wanted to hear what she had to say for herself. He'd lost his mom to cancer at fifteen years old, and he couldn't respect anyone who tried to end their life. It was a cowardly way out.

The door to her room opened and a young doctor with a receding hairline stepped out, clipboard in hand. "You can see her now. She's still not one hundred percent, so go easy on her. You only have a few minutes. She needs her rest."

Brody nodded, nausea rising in his gut as he stepped into Madison's room. His gaze went straight to the woman in the hospital bed, her hair fanned beneath her, an IV in her arm, dullness in her eyes. She didn't bother to smile as he approached.

As he touched the metal bed railing, he cleared his throat. "Madison."

She nodded. "Detective Philips."

"I need to write up a report."

She touched the sensitive skin around her neck and looked toward the window. Her hand then moved to her temple until finally she looked at him. "I'm sorry. I don't think the drugs have worn off yet. My mind is…not right."

She'd taken drugs before hanging herself? Had the medication not worked fast enough? He'd never understand some people. He pulled out his notebook and a pen, and tried to keep any judgment out of his voice. It wasn't like he had any room to judge anyone, not after everything he'd done. "Drugs, you said? What did you take?"

Some of the dullness left her eyes and she straightened slightly. Her gaze fully focused on him now. "What did I *take?* I didn't *take* anything. A man injected me with something."

Brody rotated his shoulders back. "A man?"

"You thought I was trying to kill myself?"

"There was a suicide note." His gut instinct had been right. There was more to this story. Had her attacker been in the house when he had broken in? He had to tell the sheriff, get the deputies to start a search. Maybe there was some evidence that hadn't been destroyed by the crew of paramedics, firefighters and sheriff's deputies roaming her place.

"The man—the monster—forced me to write the note. Had a knife to my throat." She closed her eyes, as if the memory physically hurt. When she opened them, Brody saw the pain there. "I thought I was going to die. If you hadn't come when you did…"

He cleared his throat. "Can you tell me anything about the man who did this to you?"

"He wore a black mask. Medium height. Thin,

but strong. His shoes were dirty. Dusty almost. I think…I think his eyes were brown. His voice was disguised."

"Disguised how? By an electronic voice modulator?"

"No, it just sounded like he was trying to make his voice deeper as he spoke."

"His voice didn't sound familiar?"

She shook her head. "No, not at all."

Brody sat down in the chair at her bedside. "I know it's going to be difficult, but I need you to tell me everything that happened. Every detail will be important."

The door opened and the same young doctor strode inside. "Not right now. She needs to rest. Her body has been through serious trauma and she needs to recover. She can answer your questions later."

Brody stood. "Time is of the essence here, doc. The more time that passes, the less likely it is that we'll find this guy."

"You'll be the first person we tell when she's rested up. But now I've got to insist that you leave."

Brody looked back at Madison and saw her eyes were closed. Reluctantly, he nodded and stepped from the room. He'd wait outside the door until she woke. In the meantime, he'd get a crime-scene crew out to her house to look for evidence.

Who would do this to someone like Madison? He didn't intend to slow down until he found out.

When Madison awoke again, her head pounded. She'd hoped the events of the day were simply a terrible nightmare, but the beeping of the heart monitor and the IV attached to her arm proved that the attack had been all too real. Tears filled her eyes, followed by relief that she'd survived and anger that the attack had happened at all.

"Reid," she whispered. Life had been so much easier when she'd had someone to share her burdens with. It still didn't seem fair that her husband had been taken from her so early. They'd had so much of life left to share together.

The drugs still made her mind feel sluggish, made her emotions harder to reign in. Her eyelids still drooped. Her limbs felt heavy.

Brody's face floated into her thoughts. Thank goodness for her neighbor. Though he'd not even given her the time of day since he'd moved in, at least he'd been there when she'd needed him.

Madison had been put off when she'd first introduced herself to him. She'd only wanted to make the newcomer feel welcome in the neighborhood. But the man had acted as if she had made a pass at him and he'd wanted to send a clear "not interested" message. Sure, the man was handsome. Any woman would think so. He had thick, dark brown hair, even features, broad shoulders and towered at least six feet tall. He'd reminded her a bit of a Ken doll, which she didn't find necessarily complimentary. Brody almost appeared too plastic, his eyes too lifeless.

Besides, Madison hadn't for a single minute been interested in another man since Reid died. She knew the kind of love they had was a once-in-a-lifetime experience. To find someone else who shared her faith in God, who understood her and respected her the way her late husband had didn't seem like even a remote possibility. What they'd felt for each other had been beautiful and when Lincoln was born, life had seemed perfect.

Lincoln.

Her gaze darted the room, searching for a clock. Three thirty. Someone needed to pick up Lincoln from preschool. She had to call someone to get him.

She swung her hand toward the phone on her nightstand, but her fingers fumbled. The device crashed to the floor with a loud jangle of metal and plastic.

She threw her feet over the side of the bed. Her IV tugged at her wrist, the medical tape pulling at her skin. Her entire body felt like it might topple out of bed.

Momentum seemed to pull her toward the floor and the room began to spin. Just then the door burst open. Brody rushed toward her. His strong hands caught her shoulders and eased her back into the hospital bed before she hit the floor.

"What are you doing?"

She pushed her head into her pillow, praying the wave of dizziness would pass. "Lincoln. My son. Someone needs to pick him up from preschool. He's going to be scared, think I forgot him."

He cleared his throat. "I asked my cousin to pick him up for you."

Madison's mind raced. "Kayla?" Kayla was one of Lincoln's preschool teachers and also went to church with them. The two had recently struck up a friendship, but it was still new, not the kind of friendship where you asked for favors yet.

"I know you two know each other, so I figured you'd trust her. I do."

Madison did trust Kayla and so did Lincoln. That was the important thing. She didn't want her son to be freaked out by everything that had happened. "How'd you know someone needed to pick him up?"

"I'm a detective. I'm paid to be observant."

"He can't go to our home. Or see me like this. I

should call her..." Her thoughts crashed into one another. She again started to reach for the phone, but Brody eased her back toward the bed.

"Don't worry. I asked her to take him to the park and to get some ice cream. He can stay with her as long as needed. You'll probably be discharged today. You can both stay with her if you need to. I know she'd be more than happy to help out with Lincoln. Don't tell her I told you, but I'm pretty sure he's her favorite student. She talks about him all the time. Those kids are her life."

Some of the tension left Madison's shoulders. Kayla's bubbly personality connected with the preschoolers in her class, and since she was single and had no children of her own, her students did seem to be her life. "Wow. You thought of everything. Thank you."

He shrugged. "I just tried to put myself in your shoes."

"I appreciate it."

He glanced toward the door before looking back at her, a professional uptightness replacing his earlier sympathy. "Listen, I know the doctor hasn't freed you to talk with me, but do you feel up to going over what happened?"

She pushed herself up, trying to ignore her aching body as she gathered her wits. Did she really want to relive what had happened? "I just want to forget."

"Forgetting won't get this man behind bars."

She touched the tender area around her neck, remembered the feeling of the rope there. Was it even possible to forget? Probably not. She was going to have to face this head-on if she ever hoped to move past it. Her hands trembled as she placed them in her lap.

She glanced at the detective and nodded. "Okay. I'm ready."

THREE

Madison's fingers twisted the white blanket covering her. Her nails dug into the threads with enough force that the fabric separated and her fingertips scraped her legs. She twisted the blanket over and over as she tried to get a handle on her thoughts.

The detective stood at her bedside, his green eyes, framed with thick lashes, looking at her intently. Each muscle in his body looked rigid as he stood poised to take notes on what she told him. If not for the flash of compassion she saw in the depths of his gaze every once in a while, she might feel intimidated.

She had to get this over with. Share her story, do her part, then pick up her son and try to resume normal life.

She'd learned how to make a new "normal" after her husband had died. She knew she could do it again. She had to. With Lincoln, she didn't have much choice. Sitting around and feeling sorry for herself wasn't an option if she wanted her son to have a happy childhood.

"Ma'am?" The detective's voice sounded soft but urgent.

Her gaze met the detective's again. She licked her lips and nodded, forcing herself to relax her hand against the blanket. "Sorry. I don't know where to start."

"Not to sound like I'm speaking in clichés, but just start at the beginning."

"The beginning." She sucked in a deep breath and noted that even her lungs ached for some reason. "I guess it all started when I walked in from dropping my son off at preschool. As soon as I stepped inside my house I heard something ticking."

He raised an eyebrow. "Like a bomb?"

She shook her head and immediately regretted it as the room began spinning again. She closed her eyes until regaining her equilibrium. "It was one of those little plastic timers people use in the kitchen. Not the digital kind…the old-fashioned kind. I thought my son had left it on. I found the timer in the bathroom, turned it off and tossed it in a drawer. After my shower, I heard it ticking again. When I went into the bathroom to turn it off, I spotted a man waiting for me." She pulled in a shaky breath, but the air didn't fill her lungs.

She sucked in more breaths as fear threatened to overtake her.

"You okay?"

The image of the man hiding in her shower flashed into her mind and her body began trembling uncontrollably. Trying to stop the tremors was useless, so she pushed forward, knowing she had no other choice. "He put a knife to my throat. Before I could even react, he injected something into my arm. I got drowsy right away." She rubbed her arm, her fingers still shaking. She could still feel the sting of the needle and the burn of the injection.

Detective Philips placed his hand over hers, bringing her back to reality. The jolt of electricity she felt at his touch shocked her, and she drew back.

His hand moved to the bed railing. "Are you sure you're okay? I can get the doctor in here."

"I'm fine. It…it just seems surreal." She crossed her arms over her chest. "He told me to go into my office. I did. At my desk, he dictated a note to me. Said he'd kill me and my son if I didn't write it. So I did."

"Did he recite the note as if he'd rehearsed it? Or did he wing it?"

She closed her eyes, everything still so vivid. "He pulled a piece of paper from his pocket, unfolded it and read it to me. He was very precise on what I should say. I couldn't miss a word."

"What happened next?"

"As soon as I signed my name to the note, he dragged me into my bedroom, reached under my bed and pulled out a rope. He must have planted the noose there when I was out." She shuddered at the thought of someone watching her house, knowing her routine and using it to plan his crime.

"You're doing great, Madison."

His encouragement gave her the strength to keep going when she'd like nothing more than to stop. The next few minutes had been horrific. She'd been certain her life would end. "He made me tie the rope to the fan. He already had it looped up. Everything was planned and ready…" Her voiced cracked.

"Do you need to take a break?"

"No. I just want to finish." Her throat suddenly felt dry. The emotions from the event rushed back to her, but she fought them. "I realized he was going to kill me," she croaked out. "Whatever he injected into me made me feel like with each movement I made I was swimming through gelatin. I kept thinking of Lincoln." Her voice caught and she grabbed a tissue to dab her eyes.

"He seems like a great boy."

She nodded. "Yes, he is. I knew I had to fight

this man, that once I had that rope around my neck my chances of surviving would diminish. I elbowed the man in the nose. He threw me into my dresser. I hit my head and everything really started to spin."

"It was obvious you put up a good fight. You probably didn't stand a chance since he drugged you."

"What did he give me?" she asked.

"We're still doing a tox screen now. We'll know soon."

She sucked in a breath, wanting to block out the memories, but knowing she couldn't. The sound of the man's voice, the feel of his gloved hands grabbing her wrists, the image of his glistening knife all flashed back.

"I didn't have much energy after that. He grabbed me, wrapped the noose around my neck and put that stool under me just to taunt me. My feet could barely touch it, just enough to suck in a breath every once in a while. Plus the drugs were knocking me out. It was just a matter of time. I knew I was dead."

"What did the man do next?"

"I heard a crash from the front of the house. It must have been you. The man ran to the bathroom. Must have jumped out the window." She wiped the tears from her eyes again. "Have I said thank you enough?"

"I'm glad I was jogging when I was."

"You're a godsend."

"No one's ever said that God sent me before. Usually the opposite." He smiled mischievously.

"I don't know about that."

His smile disappeared. "Madison, think about this carefully. When the man ran, did he look panicked?"

She thought about it a moment. "Not really. He seemed relatively calm. Of course, I was fighting for my life, so I wasn't paying as much attention to him at that point. Is that really important, detective?"

"It gives me insight into the man's mindset. Every detail helps." Brody met her eyes. "You have no idea who this man was, do you? No enemies or anyone who would want to harm you?"

She shook her head. "No, not that I know of."

He shifted his weight to his other foot. "Tell me about this timer."

"There's not much to say about it. My attacker seemed to be taunting me with it. At first I assumed the ticking was coming from one of my son's toys or that Lincoln had been playing with the timer and left it on. I knew deep down when I heard the ticking the second time that something was wrong."

Brody started to ask another question when the doctor burst into the room. "Detective, I don't recall giving you permission to come in here." The doctor scowled at Brody as he walked briskly to Madison's bedside.

"I dropped something and he came in to help," Madison jumped in, feeling a strange need to defend the man who, up until today, had seemed opposed to even giving a neighborly hello. "He did nothing wrong."

The doctor didn't look convinced as he stared at Brody through his wire-framed glasses and tapped his finger impatiently against a clipboard. "I need a moment to examine my patient."

Brody nodded and looked back at Madison. "Thanks for your time. I'll be in touch. And if you think of anything in the meantime..."

"I know where to find you."

With another clipped nod, he left the room. Madison immediately missed his presence. Something about just having him in the room made her feel safer, as if everything would somehow work out. That same chill from earlier returned and she again faced the situation...alone.

Something about what Madison told him nagged at Brody. As he left her hospital room, he mentally replayed the conversation with her, trying to pinpoint whatever it was that seemed to be clamoring at him to take notice. Whatever it was remained on the edge of his rationing, taunting him.

Brody waited in the hospital hallway until a deputy showed up to guard the door to Madison's room before he went home to shower and dress. Most likely the killer wouldn't be foolish enough to come to the hospital and finish what he'd started, but Brody wanted to be safe. Until they had a profile of this man, he'd take every precaution necessary.

He needed to get to the station and talk to the sheriff, but first he needed to change out of his shorts and T-shirt. He gripped the steering wheel of his sedan as he turned off the highway and onto a more rural road leading toward his home. The glaring sun, unhindered by his visor, only further served to agitate him. What was it about Madison's story that nagged at him?

As he pulled into his driveway, he saw that the emergency crew was gone from Madison's. Looking at her home now, one would never have guessed the tragedy that had almost transpired there. Inside would certainly be a different story. He intended on reviewing the evidence inside her home himself after he checked in with the sheriff.

He quickly showered and changed into khakis and a blue, button-up shirt. Twenty minutes later he arrived at the neat, two-story station, his car crunching the gravel in the parking lot. As he looked at the brick-fronted building, he shook his head. What a change this place was compared to the precinct he worked at in Brooklyn.

"The sheriff in yet?" he asked Miranda, the deputy working the front desk.

She glanced up over the red frames perched on her nose. "Not yet. They're finishing up that accident on the highway. Should be back anytime now."

"Thanks," he mumbled, grabbing a cup of stale coffee on the way past.

He nodded an aloof greeting to his colleagues before reaching his office. Once in his well-used swivel chair, he stared at his desk a moment. Where to start on this one? With typing up the police report, he supposed. Then he'd have to check in with the crime-scene crew to see what they'd found. Hopefully any additional evidence hadn't been trampled.

Halfway through typing his report, he stopped. There'd been two other suicides in York County in the past few months. York County wasn't a huge place. What was the probability that the area had had two suicides within a four-month period?

He wanted to look through those files again. They'd seemed open-and-closed enough at the time. But what if there was more to those cases than they'd first assumed? Brody found the reports he needed and began reviewing the information.

The first suicide had happened in May. The man, Willie Fisher, was a mechanic. He worked for a local auto repair shop off Route 17, the main highway through York County. Two weeks before his death, Willie had been fired from his job for supposedly stealing money from the company. He'd claimed his innocence, but his reputation had taken a beating. He'd even gone to the doctor and been prescribed medicine for depression only three days before his life ended through carbon-monoxide poisoning.

The second suicide was a young sheriff's deputy named Victor Hanson who'd died in June. He'd just graduated from the academy a year earlier and seemed to have a promising career within the department. His wife had left him prior to his death. Victor's suicide note alluded to the pain of her rejection being too much to take. He'd taken a gun to his head.

Brody had actually bought his truck from Willie and he'd seen the man on occasion at the gym he frequented off Route 17. And, of course, he knew Victor from the Sheriff's Department. Brody marveled how connected everyone was in a small town. This place was so much different than New York.

He stared at the reports. Was there something here that he was missing? Could these deaths have been more than suicides? Could those men have been murdered? And, if so, what was the tie between their murders and the attempted murder of Madison?

He couldn't get the agonized look she'd had out of his mind. She'd handled the situation well and drawn from a deep strength within herself, one that impressed him. Even as she'd recalled the horrid details of what had happened, she'd seemed to have a peace about her. The woman, even in her battered state, was certainly beautiful. She was the type of woman who could turn heads and not even realize it. Petite and trim with blue eyes that matched the bay. Not that he'd noticed, he told himself.

"How's Madison doing?" Sheriff Carl appeared behind him, his brow still damp with sweat from being in the stifling heat outside. Brody often marveled that Sheriff Carl looked exactly like Andy Griffith from his later years on the TV show *Matlock*.

Brody swiveled in his chair and decided not to mince words. "Sheriff, this wasn't a suicide like we first assumed. Madison said a man attacked her and forced her to write that suicide note before attempting to murder her."

The sheriff's eyes widened, as if in shock, before he slowly nodded. "I knew she wasn't capable of suicide, especially not with that boy of hers. He means everything to her. She wouldn't leave him."

"This crime was calculated, Sheriff. Every last detail was planned, all the way down to using her egg timer to count down the minutes until he attacked her. He had a suicide note already written and the noose stocked under her bed. The only thing he didn't plan on was that I'd be jogging and hear Madison scream."

Sheriff Carl, a man whom Brody had come to respect because of his even temperament and measured wisdom, nodded again, obviously soaking in all of the information Brody threw at him.

"Do you usually jog at the same time every day?"

"No, sir. I usually jog as the sun comes up. But since today was officially my day off, I decided to sleep in." Not to mention that he couldn't sleep last night because he'd had nightmares of Lindsey, about his old life back in New York. And like every nightmare he'd beaten himself up through, the ending was always the same. He'd woken up covered in sweat, laden with guilt and uncertain of his ability to ever change into a better man.

"So your routine was off. The suspect was probably counting on you jogging this morning as you always do."

"Sounds accurate to me."

"Madison's a sweet girl. I hate to think of her going through this. Her husband was a good man, a true patriot. For someone to target a widow with a young child is just beyond me. Of course, sometimes I think this whole world has gone mad."

"Sometimes it feels like it has, sir."

Sheriff Carl glanced at the papers and files covering Brody's desk. "What are you looking at?"

"Those other two suicides we've had here in York County recently."

"You think there's a connection?"

"I need to investigate the cases, Sheriff. I don't believe in coincidences."

"You've got a good instinct. Go with it. I have to say, I hope you're wrong. If you're not, that means there's a serial killer on the loose here in York County." He sighed heavily. "The whole county will go crazy if that leaks out. Let's not say anything until we know for sure."

"Got it."

Brody couldn't help but think that maybe the whole county should be going crazy. Until this man was caught, no one was safe.

Especially not Madison.

FOUR

A sheriff's deputy drove Madison to Kayla's house. Madison was forever grateful to Bonnie, Sheriff Carl's wife, who brought her some clean clothes and a few toiletries. The last thing Madison had wanted was for Lincoln to see her in her previous state: torn shirt, disheveled hair, busted lip. He'd already been through enough. No need to traumatize him further.

She sat silently in the front seat as the rookie deputy rolled down the quiet streets toward Seaford. How could such an attack have happened in such a peaceful little fishing community? She'd always felt safe here. It was against her instincts to leave her doors unlocked, but she knew people who did and she understood their reasoning. The worst crime that usually happened here was a drunk driver or a brawl between neighbors. Nothing like what had happened to her today. As soon as the news media found out it wasn't an attempted suicide, they'd be on the story like a crab on seaweed. The fact that she freelanced for the newspaper wouldn't give her any immunity.

"Can I stop and get you anything, ma'am?" Deputy Young asked kindly.

She shook her head. "No, I just want to see my son. Thank you, though." She twisted the tissue in her hand until it ripped. Looking at her lap and the evidence of her anguished thoughts, she collected the scraps of tissue and stuffed the pieces into her pocket.

Her thoughts drifted to Brody. She wished he was with her now instead of the fresh-faced deputy. There was something she'd found comforting today about the man and his demeanor.

She wondered about the torment she'd briefly seen on his face as she'd recounted the details of her attack. She'd thought, just for a moment, that she'd seen something very raw flash through his gaze. The grueling emotions she'd spotted seemed to be deeper than those of a compassionate detective. What about her attack made him look regretful?

The man had a heart. She shouldn't be surprised. Kayla—his cousin and Lincoln's teacher—had expressed that much, saying that Madison shouldn't let his aloofness bother her. She'd insisted he was going through some stuff that had left him in a bit of an identity crisis. Ignoring his typical blatant disregard of her was easier said than done, however. But now this new side of him emerged, and Madison didn't know what to think about Brody Philips.

Finally the car pulled to a stop in front of Kayla's bungalow, a small yellow house that sat on a stretch of other similar houses on a lone country road. The deputy started to walk her to the door, but Madison politely declined. Before she made it even halfway up the sidewalk, the front door flew open and little blond haired Lincoln ran out to greet her. With his trim, lean frame and blue eyes, he was the spitting image of his father. The feel of his sticky hands around her neck made her forget everything else, even the searing pain that ripped through her ribs.

He pulled his head back and looked at her from only four inches away. "Mommy, where were you? I thought we were going to the playground today."

The playground. She'd totally forgotten about her promise to him. "We'll go this week. I promise. Mommy had a little…accident and isn't feeling very well."

Her son studied her face with a frown. "Did you catch a germ?"

Madison smiled. "Not quite. Don't you worry, though. I'm doing much better now that I'm with you."

Kayla smiled from the doorway. As Madison

carried Lincoln up the steps, she waved at the deputy and he drove away. Kayla extended her arm behind her, welcoming Madison inside. Still holding Lincoln, Madison stepped into the cool living room, grateful to get out of the smothering heat.

Kayla closed the door and offered a warm smile. "I made some Boatman's Stew, in case you're hungry. Lincoln already had some pizza. I hope that's okay."

Madison nodded and touched her throat. "Of course." When would this stop feeling so surreal? Images continually flashed back into her mind, making her feel like she could hardly breathe.

"Mom, can I finish my video game?"

Madison nodded and the boy scrambled back to the TV, picked up a remote and began playing an alphabet game. Madison followed Kayla's lead and settled on the couch, unsure of what to do with herself.

Madison looked at the petite woman across from her. Kayla was probably only a few years younger than Madison and had a square face, a sprinkle of freckles across her cheeks, and lovely, thick auburn hair. "How's Lincoln been?"

"He's been great. He's asked a lot of questions, but really he's such an easygoing kid. I didn't tell him anything. I figured you'd want to handle that."

"I appreciate everything you've done," Madison said.

"I just...I just can't believe something like this would happen here...and to you." Kayla shook her head. "I'm so sorry you're going through this."

"I'm still in a state of disbelief myself."

A knock sounded at the door. Kayla disappeared and a moment later Madison heard a deep voice echoing from the front door. Her heart sped slightly when she realized it was Brody. She scolded herself for the reaction.

He'd saved her life. Of course she might have the man at hero status for now. It wouldn't last long. Soon he'd return to being her grouchy neighbor and she'd resume her routine as a single working mom. The only reason he showed so much concern now was because of his job—he had no choice but to be kind.

She rose, rubbing her hands against her jeans, as his broad form filled the doorway. "Brody."

He nodded toward her, his posture stiff and professional. "Madison. I just thought I'd stop by and see how you're doing."

"Kayla's been a lifesaver." She glanced back at Lincoln, who still played a video game, oblivious to anything that had happened. "We're all hanging in, doing as well as can be expected."

His eyes caught hers, and he seemed to search her gaze for evidence of truth in her words. She looked away, afraid he'd seen her fear and exhaustion.

He seemed to take the hint as the warmth left his eyes and an aloof professionalism replaced it. "I wanted to let you know that the crime scene has been cleared. You're free to return home whenever you're ready."

Kayla placed her hand on Madison's arm. Compassionate eyes met hers. "You're welcome to stay here for as long as you need."

Madison nodded, relief filling her. She wasn't sure she was ready to face her house yet. Though Bonnie had also offered them the chance to stay at her place, Madison knew that Bonnie's ailing mother also lived there. Madison didn't want to place any more pressure on the woman. Kayla's place would be perfect, though, especially since Lincoln already felt at home here. "I appreciate it. I think I'll go back to my house tomorrow after Lincoln is at school and try to straighten up. I don't want him to see it in its current state." The noose wrapped around the fan flashed into her mind. She squeezed her eyes shut, trying to erase the image.

A firm hand came down on her shoulder. She opened her eyes and saw that Brody had closed the distance between them. The warmth returned to his gaze.

"That's probably a good idea." His voice sounded kind and assuring. Her racing thoughts slowed. "How about if I pick you up in the morning to help out? You're going to need a new front door. I'd be happy to help replace it, especially since I was the one who knocked it down."

Madison felt her eyes widen against her will. Was this the same man who'd given her the cold shoulder since he'd moved in? Again she reminded herself that he was just doing his job—though fixing her door probably wasn't written out explicitly in his work description. "I don't want you to go out of your way…"

"I don't mind."

She swallowed, her throat dry. "Thank you, then. That would be a huge help."

His hand dropped from her shoulder and she instantly missed it. Was she this desperate for someone to help take care of her? She'd never thought of herself as a needy woman. Instead, she'd thought she'd been strong and independent. Based on her reactions to Brody today, maybe she was wrong.

Brody gave her a tight smile before nodding at Kayla. "Good night, then. Call me if you need anything. And lock your doors tonight."

Madison shuddered. Did locked doors even keep people safe? Today had proved otherwise.

As Brody drove home, he wondered why he'd volunteered to spend more time than necessary with Madison. He told himself it was because she might remember more details about her attacker and Brody wanted to be there when she did. He even told himself that it was his job to keep her safe, although in actuality his job was to solve the crime more than act as bodyguard.

Brody knew there was more to his offer. He'd known from the moment he set eyes on the pretty blonde that she was the type of woman it would be easy to fall for. If he was smart, he'd still keep her at a distance. He'd let her find someone from church or work who could help her with the door. He'd interact with her only enough to get the answers he needed, he decided as he pulled up in front of his house.

But if he didn't help her pick up in the aftermath of the attack, who would? The woman seemed so busy that he rarely saw her take time for social visits at her home. Not that he was paying attention to who came and went.

He glanced over at her house, unusually silent and dark without Madison and Lincoln inside. Okay, maybe sometimes he did pay attention to what went on at his neighbor's. He couldn't help it. Anyone coming or going did have to pass his home first since the street dead ended past her house.

Keep your distance, he warned himself again.

He let himself into his quiet home, one so very different from his apartment in Brooklyn. He'd never dreamed he'd be in a place like Seaford or that he'd enjoy the small town as he did. Still, he didn't plan on being here forever. It was better if he didn't get to know his neighbor—or anybody else, for that matter—too well.

The last thing he wanted to do was to ruin someone else's life. He already had a long enough of list of people whose lives he'd messed up. Especially Lindsey...

Just the thought of her made a heaviness settle over him. It happened every time she crossed his mind. He'd never forgive himself for his past mistakes. Never. Yet here he was thinking about his pretty neighbor.

That settled it. Tomorrow he would do as he'd promised and fix her door. But after that he'd do his job and nothing more.

Madison shook off her chills as she stood on the front porch of Kayla's house the next morning. The August heat felt stifling, yet still she shivered. Her gaze traveled from side to side again, searching the shrubs decorating Kayla's flower beds. It would be a while before she stopped looking around every corner for an intruder. Experiences—traumas—like yesterday would take months, maybe years, to get past. Or would she ever get past it? She shook her head. Of course she would. With a little bit of trust in God she could overcome anything, even this enormous mountain before her.

Kayla had left thirty minutes ago for work at the preschool and had taken Lincoln with her. Brody had told Madison he'd pick her up this morning and go with her into her home. She was incredibly grateful for his support. The idea of facing her home alone made her stomach roil. Even if it was just Brody and if he was just doing his job, having him there would ease her apprehension some. She'd take whatever she could get.

She swatted away a gnat and glanced at her watch again. She still had five minutes until he arrived. Five long minutes. She looked around the porch once more, making sure she hadn't missed any creepy indications that she should be on guard. Nothing. She should feel relieved. Why didn't she?

Madison had stayed inside Kayla's home for the first twenty minutes after her gracious hostess had left for work. But every creak and groan of the house had made her practically jump out of her skin. She'd decided that being out here on the wide, open porch would allow her to feel safer.

But would she ever feel safe again? Why did that question continually come back to her? Why couldn't her logic and emotions work hand in hand? Instead, they often seemed at odds with each other.

She shook her head, which started to ache. She had to put those thoughts out of her mind. Life was going on and for Lincoln's sake she had to keep up. There was no time to feel sorry for herself.

A truck coming down the road caught her attention. She straightened, held her breath a moment. Brody? Why did the thought of seeing him cause a tingle of excitement to race up her spine? She scolded herself for even feeling anything. She had so much to worry about already. She had no room in her life for romance.

Brody's broad frame filled the government-issued vehicle. In a few minutes, that same imposing frame would help her to feel protected when she ventured back through the scene of her attack.

The truck pulled to a stop at the end of Kayla's driveway, and Brody stepped out. A tense smile greeted her. She didn't wait for Brody to reach the porch. She started toward him, ready to get this over with.

"Morning," he mumbled.

She only glanced at him long enough to nod her hello. "Good morning, Brody."

He opened the passenger-side door for her and waited for her to slide in. Once seated and buckled in, Madison scrutinized the interior of the vehicle. It was everything she'd expected from Brody—orderly, neat and without any bells or whistles.

He slid in beside her a moment later and the scent of spearmint filled the vehicle. He wore a golf shirt and jeans. Not the typical attire she expected from a detective, but Madison knew he planned on helping at her home today.

"How are you feeling today?"

"Achy, tired, grateful. Everything you'd expect, I suppose." She rubbed her neck, still remembering the feeling of the rope there. Her skin was still raw and bruised, and wouldn't let her forget.

"It will get easier with time."

"I know." She sighed and pulled her arms across her chest as they cruised down the road. "Any leads?"

"Not yet. But we're looking at what happened from every angle."

"I can't believe that monster is still out there." She shivered again. "When he finds out I survived, do you think he'll…?" The rest of the words wouldn't leave her lips. She didn't want to say them aloud. Couldn't bear to.

Brody glanced over at her and something flickered in his eyes. What was it? Fear for her safety? The realization that Madison couldn't avoid the truth? The thought that she was simply paranoid, perhaps in shock after yesterday's events?

"He'd be foolish to come back," Brody finally said.

Madison noticed he didn't say that her would-be killer wouldn't come back, though. Her head throbbed.

"You okay?"

She nodded and stared out the window. The thought of her attacker coming back to finish what he'd started made panic churn in her gut and rip apart every shred of peace she tried to hold on to. Her hands began to shake, tears welled in her eyes and images from yesterday began playing rapid fire in her head.

A hand clamped down on her knee. "Hey."

Madison swung her head toward the voice. Brody. Just Brody.

"I'm going to keep an eye on you, make sure you stay safe. It's going to be okay."

"I wish I felt so certain." What about Lincoln? What if the man came back and tried to harm her son? She couldn't bear the thought of it. Perhaps she should simply take Lincoln and go somewhere, anywhere. Maybe down to see her parents in Florida? On that vacation to the Bahamas that she'd been dreaming about?

Vacation was out. She barely had money to pay her bills. Not to mention she'd be getting another bill—a hospital bill—soon. Though her insurance would pay for most of it, how much would her portion be? How would she ever pay for that?

She could stay with her parents, but her dad had a heart condition. If he found out what had happened, his blood pressure might rise and trigger more problems with his heart. She could never live with herself if she caused something to happen to her dad.

"We'll catch him, Madison." Brody's voice sounded confident, reassuring. It was as if he could read her mind.

Just then they pulled up to her house.

With each step she took toward her backdoor, nausea rumbled in her gut. Could she face this nightmare again? She swallowed as they stepped inside, trying to stay strong. Brody led her to the foyer.

Madison grabbed the wall as the room began to sway. Or was that her swaying? She couldn't be sure. Perhaps she should have asked a friend to be here with her, to help her walk through this.

Instead, Brody stood at her side, and he looked as if he'd rather be waiting in line at the DMV than walking through her emotions with her.

A huge piece of plywood was nailed where the front door used to be. Now that she stood in the place where her nightmare had begun, she soaked in all the details. Splintered, cracked wood littered the tile floor in front of her while exposed timber gaped at the door jamb. There were her keys on the table, just where she'd left them. Who knew the nightmare that she was about to encounter when she'd deposited her keys there and gone to get dressed for the day. The act had seemed so simple and ordinary, but right now, as she looked at those keys, she remembered again how quickly life could change.

Yesterday flashed into her mind. She'd been in such a hurry to make her photography appointments. She remembered the sound of ticking. She halfway expected to hear it again. But all was quiet. So quiet she could hear her heartbeat.

"It's too soon for you, isn't it? I should have told you to stay away for a while."

"I have to face the house sometime. It might as well be today." If only she felt as confident as her words sounded. Her body betrayed her and sagged against the wall.

Brody's hand cupped her elbow. "Anytime you want to stop, you just let me know."

She nodded. "Do you know how he got in yet? I always lock the house up."

"There's no evidence of forced entry, no jimmy marks on the windows or doors, no broken screens or locks. Is there anywhere someone might have gotten a copy of your house key?"

She shook her head. "I keep one on my key

ring and one hidden in my car." She'd used the one in her car to get inside her home today—it had still been just where she'd left it. So apparently her attacker was a phantom who could creep through walls. The thought didn't comfort her.

"Do you always leave your car unlocked, like it was today?"

Heat filled her cheeks. Locking her home seemed safe and logical, but she never even thought twice about leaving her car unlocked. "I do."

"Nobody else has a copy of the house key? A boyfriend or relative maybe?"

"My parents don't live in the area and I have no time for a boyfriend, so, no." Her words reminded her of how much life had changed in the past three years. Her parents had decided to retire and move to Florida six months before her husband had died in an auto accident. Suddenly, there was no one. Just her and Lincoln. Life had gone from being full of love and family to being a struggle.

"How about if we take a break? We'll go into town and get you a new door. We'll get the entire foyer cleaned up before we tackle anything else."

Madison nodded, grateful for his suggestion because she was beginning to feel suffocated in her own home.

FIVE

After picking out a door at the closest hardware store, the two headed back to Madison's house. The ride was mainly quiet. She wasn't in the state of mind to come up with polite small talk, and Brody didn't seem like the type who ever used nonsensical conversation. So instead, Madison stared out the window, wishing desperately that her thoughts had an escape hatch. No such luck.

"Why would someone do something like that?" Madison's words surprised even her.

Brody gripped the steering wheel as if trying to find the right words. "Your guess is as good as mine. Some people just get their kicks by causing other people pain. It's sad, but it's reality."

"You really think this was just some random crime intended to simply entertain a criminal?"

He shrugged. "Nothing was stolen. The setup was elaborate and required thought beforehand. What other motive would there be except that he was sick? A psychologist would probably give some mumbo jumbo about the suspect's messed up childhood or a twisted need for revenge because they were bullied in high school. I hate that rationale because it seems to try and justify the behavior." He exhaled sharply. "I just think some people are messed up. Call them psycho if you want. Insane. Evil. But don't try and make me feel sorry for them. We're all responsible for own actions."

She shook her head. "So let's say this was a rational but evil man who did this. If he wanted to kill me, then why not just kill me? If he wanted to torture me, then why not just torture me then kill me? But this man had a plan—a very specific plan, I'd say based on the note he had me write and the way he knew my schedule. It doesn't make sense to me."

"More details will come to light with time, Madison. My colleagues at the Sheriff's Department are working on the case now. It's too early to make any assumptions."

"This area always seemed so safe."

"Crime happens everywhere," Brody reminded her.

"I guess you've seen your fair share of crimes. You came down from New York City, right?"

"I did," he said with a nod.

"You don't have the accent."

He smiled. "I didn't grow up there. My parents are actually from here. My dad and Kayla's dad are brothers. My dad joined the military after high school, so I spent my childhood living all over the world."

"Military brat, huh?"

"Yeah. It wasn't too bad, though. I kind of liked being exposed to different parts of the country and world. I think living in different places made me a better person."

She looked at him curiously. "How did you end up in New York?"

"I figured if I was going to become a cop, I might as well do it somewhere exciting. So I applied in the Big Apple, and I got the job."

"Seaford has to be quite the change for you. It's probably like a different world."

"It is," he agreed. "But change is good."

Madison's cell phone buzzed. She didn't recognize the number on her screen, but that wasn't unusual with her job. Perhaps it was another client she'd forgotten to reschedule? She flipped her phone open and saw an incoming message. A moment later a picture popped up on her screen.

Madison gasped and the phone tumbled from her hands. Her heart sped as sweat dotted her forehead. That couldn't have been... Had she imagined the picture? Why would someone...?

"Madison, what's wrong?"

She pointed toward the floor, between her feet. "I…there…on my phone."

Brody pulled off the road, put the truck into park and reached down to the floor to retrieve her phone.

Madison squeezed the skin between her eyes. She couldn't get the image from her mind. It was a picture of her, hanging from the ceiling fan. Her eyes had been closed, as if death had already claimed her. Her attacker must have taken the picture, but she couldn't remember him doing so. So much about yesterday was a blur, though. The drugs made everything fuzzy and unclear.

Who could be so evil and cruel to do these things to her?

Brody stared at the phone, shaking his head. "I'll see if we can trace where this came from. Most likely whoever sent this used one of those prepaid phones. All of these crime shows on TV have made it way too easy to figure things like that out. They're making criminals smarter." He glanced over at her, his green eyes filled with compassion. "I'm sorry you had to see that, Madison."

"I guess he knows I'm still alive." She shivered and sunk down in her seat, wishing the upholstery would simply swallow her so she wouldn't have to face this nightmare anymore. "What does that picture mean, though? Why would he bother contacting me now?"

"I don't know, Madison," he said gruffly.

"It's not over yet, is it?"

Brody's nonanswer spoke volumes.

How would she keep her little family safe? If locks wouldn't keep this man out of her home, how would she ever protect herself and Lincoln?

"I'll make sure we have someone patrolling your home." Brody seemed to read her thoughts.

But someone patrolling outside her home would only bring her a temporary comfort. She wouldn't feel truly safe until this man was behind bars.

Brody started back down the road and a few minutes later they were back at her home. Brody hauled the door from his truck, propped it on his shoulder and started toward the porch.

Madison followed behind, unsure of what to do. Help him? Get out of his way? "Do you need me to do anything?"

He leaned the door against the porch. "I think I can handle this."

"If it's okay, I think I'll go to my office for a few minutes. I can't afford to take many days off of work. I need to start rescheduling some of my appointments that I missed yesterday and today."

"You going to be okay going back inside by yourself?" His gaze searched hers.

Madison nodded, though she didn't feel as confident. "Yeah, I'll be fine."

She waited until Brody had torn down the plywood on the front of her home before she ventured inside and down the hallway. Her breathing became shallow with each step she took. The door to her bedroom remained closed and she left it that way. That was the one room in her home that she wasn't prepared to face yet.

Instead she slipped into her office. Sensory images began hitting her, first of the knife at her throat, then the sound of the man's gravelly voice as he'd forced her in here and made her write that suicide note. She'd done so, afraid of upsetting him, hoping maybe she'd buy some time and figure out a way of getting out of the situation. No such luck. She'd only delayed the inevitable.

If it hadn't been for Brody...

She shook her head and gripped the edge of the desk. She couldn't let herself think like that. But obviously God did want her alive for a reason. He had a plan and purpose for her life. Her time wasn't up yet. She'd do her best to ensure it remained that way.

But if the killer had his way, would he remedy that? Would he play God again and try to end her life? Shivers racked her body.

Focus, Madison. Focus.

With shaking hands she opened her appointment book and stared at the sessions she'd missed yesterday. If she wanted to pay her bills this month, she would need to reschedule those appointments for tomorrow. She had two family-portrait sessions, baseball-team pictures for a local high school and a store opening for the newspaper. Today she'd had scheduled some headshots at a dance studio, pictures of a foster family for the newspaper and even a few properties she'd agreed to photograph for a real-estate agency.

Her favorite thing to take pictures of was the bay outside her window. But she found taking pictures of people paid better. Nature wasn't as picky about its pictures. People were. It didn't cooperate or complain or try to tell her how to set up the shot. Because she had to make money, she let her clients have the final say most of the time. After all, the customer was always right. But one day she had dreams of taking pictures of nature— God's handiwork—that she could frame and sell at local galleries. But until that dream became a reality, she only had time to take pictures that guaranteed money. If that's what it took to provide for her family, then that's what she'd do.

Sure, Reid had had life insurance. He and Madison had purchased it at the ripe old age of twenty-three. Back then they'd assumed they were both going to live forever. They'd taken out a policy that had ultimately allowed her to pay for the funeral, pay off her student loans and the remainder of her car. Certainly if they could have looked into the future, they would have planned better. But they hadn't and what was done was done. The church was kind enough to give her a discounted rate on Lincoln's preschool. Without that answered prayer, Madison didn't know how she would manage to work. Childcare was so expensive. Her parents had offered to move back up here and help her out, but Madison knew that she had to learn to stand on her own two feet. She couldn't ask her parents to give up their lives in order to help her. The idea had been tempting, however.

In the distance, she heard Brody hammering away. Hearing a man work in her home felt odd. Reid had been the handyman in the family, the one who could fix anything she needed. Since he'd died, her house didn't quite look the same. Sure, she'd learned to hang pictures halfway straight and centered, and even to change hard-to-reach light bulbs without electrocuting herself. She'd even bought a new entertainment center and managed to assemble the entire thing on her own. But if Madison was honest she'd admit that she missed having someone around to help out, to ease her burden.

She knew that no one would ever replace Reid,

though. He'd been one of a kind, her soul mate. And losing him had hurt like a piece of herself had been removed—without anesthesia or pain medication. She'd found love once, but she never wanted to open herself up to that heartache again. The pain was just too overwhelming.

She especially didn't want to open herself up to Brody, so this strange attraction she'd been feeling toward him yesterday and today needed to go away. She prided herself on keeping herself separate from her emotions, of being able to put on a brave front. She needed to draw on that now.

She sighed and picked up the phone. She might as well start making those phone calls. What did she say to her clients? *I'm sorry I missed our appointment yesterday but someone tried to kill me?* She shook her head. That would only sound absurd. She'd tell them she'd had an emergency come up. But in a town as small as Seaford, everyone had certainly already heard the whole story—at least, they'd heard someone's version of the whole story.

She'd need God's strength to get through the next few days. She knew she couldn't do it on her own.

Just as Madison hung up from her last call, a knock sounded at her office door. She looked up and saw Brody filling the doorway. The sight of him made her heart quicken again, much to her chagrin. Life was easier when she thought of the man simply as a plastic Ken doll, not as a man with compassion and kindness.

Brody nodded down the hall. "The front door is up. You want to check it out?"

"That was fast." She stood and followed him down the hallway. She was surprised at what she saw in the foyer. Not only had he put up her new door, but he'd also swept and cleaned the entire area. She could hardly tell that anything had happened there. "It looks great."

He ran his hand down the finished wood, wiping some dust from it. "A little bit of soapy water and it will practically seem like the house has had a face-lift."

She waved him off. "I think I can handle some soapy water. I just can't thank you enough for all of your help."

"I don't mind. I kind of like being handy sometimes."

She looked up at him and blanched at how close he stood. Close enough that she could smell spearmint, to see the flecks of gold in his stubble, close enough to feel overwhelmed by his size and strength. Her throat went dry and she stepped back. "Thank you, then. Let me get you a check for the door before I forget—" She took a step toward her office, but Brody grabbed her arm.

"Don't worry about it." He shrugged. "After all, I'm the reason you needed a new door."

"You broke it down so you could save my life."

"I said don't worry about it."

The way his hands went to his hips and he raised his gaze made it clear that there was no room for argument. Madison still planned on paying him back, though. She just had to do a few of these photography jobs first. She'd let his stubbornness buy her some time.

"I guess you need to get back to work now," she murmured.

His expression made it clear that he did have to go—but that he didn't want to. "I do. I need to see if we can track down whomever sent you this picture. The sooner we catch this guy, the sooner your life will return to normal."

"As normal as it can be after something like this."

"I can't argue with that." He stepped toward the door. The way he stopped there made it seem like he was almost trying to think of a reason to stay. "Madison, call me if you need anything— anything at all. Promise?"

"I do."

"Are you staying with Kayla tonight?"

Kayla had invited her to stay for as long as needed. "Probably."

"I think that's a good idea." He glanced around

the foyer again before his gaze fell on Madison. "Keep the doors locked."

"I will."

Madison stayed at the door and watched Brody as he crossed the lawn to his truck. He'd been a godsend, she couldn't deny that. It would have taken her at least a week to get someone out to fix that door if it hadn't been for him. Sure, she could have probably called someone from church or one of her friends to help her, but the truth was that her relationships had suffered since Reid died. The friends that Madison had had in the area while growing up had mostly moved away. She still knew a few people who lived in various parts of the county, but, like most parents of preschoolers, life was hectic and busy and with time they'd lost touch. Perhaps she should have tried harder, but at the end of most days she was exhausted.

After Brody disappeared into his truck, she went back to her office. She glanced out the window as she sat down. The beautiful Chesapeake Bay stared back at her. She and Reid had purchased this home while he'd been stationed down in Hampton at Langley Air Force Base. Madison had actually moved away from York County when she went to college. Then she and Reid had married. Their first station had been in Patrick Air Force Base in Florida. They'd moved back to Seaford two months before Lincoln was born. They didn't know how long Reid was going to be stationed here, but they knew this was the place they wanted to end up one day. That's why they'd purchased the small house located across the Chesapeake Bay. The home wasn't their dream home, but the location was perfect. It fed both Madison's creative side and Reid's need for space and land.

Something in the distance caught her gaze. Mr. Steinbeck, an older gentleman who'd taken to being both a school bus driver and a fisherman in his retirement, docked his boat on the bay as he did nearly every day in the summer. Locals nicknamed him Fillet since he sold fish out of his truck off the main highway through town on most days.

The man was a little different. He had a tendency to stare, probably without realizing it, but Madison could never tell what the thoughts behind the stare meant. He'd made her uncomfortable, but Reid had always insisted that the man simply didn't have many social graces. He'd lived alone for as long as Madison had known him and seemed to simply lack interpersonal skills more than anything else.

A pier jutted through the marshlands to the water, and there were a few locals whom Madison allowed to use the space. Like clockwork,

Mr. Steinbeck appeared at the pier every day around eleven o'clock to begin his excursion. And almost every day he saw Madison either coming or going. He would have had ample time to have gotten a grasp on her schedule.

Would someone like Mr. Steinbeck be responsible for committing such a despicable crime? Madison just couldn't see it. He seemed like such a gentle—albeit awkward—soul. But weren't the best criminals the ones who blended in, who tricked their victims into thinking they could do no harm?

As Madison leaned back in her office chair, she glanced outside at him again. He stood on his boat, wearing camouflage waders and a fisherman's hat. He blended right into the environment. And he was staring at her office window, almost as if he could see inside.

What if Mr. Steinbeck was more than a friendly local? What if he was behind her attack yesterday?

Chills ran up her spine at the thought, and she scooted closer to her desk and away from the open window. After yesterday she didn't know whom she could trust, and she wasn't taking any chances.

SIX

Brody didn't want to leave—yet he did. He wanted to stick close to Madison to make sure the madman who was out there stayed far away. Yet in order to catch that madman, he needed to do his job, which required him to be away from her. He'd checked out her house before he'd left to make sure everything was safe. It was. But still, her attacker had gotten in before and hardly left a trace of evidence. He could do it again.

After he showered and changed, he started down the road to the station. He decided as he drove that he would send someone over to install a security system and cameras in Madison's house. She wouldn't like it. She'd insist on paying. But he would do it, anyway—and he wouldn't accept a dime for it. After all, if he'd been a little friendlier with her when he'd moved in, then maybe he would have stopped by her house for coffee after his morning jog and deterred this lunatic from breaking in.

Those were all what-ifs. His friendship with her may have meant nothing.

Truth was none of it really mattered. His job was to solve this case, not to protect Madison. What was it about her that tugged at his heart-strings, anyway? He was usually so good at keeping his distance from the people he served. Some would say that made him a bad detective and others would say the opposite. He didn't know what he'd say anymore. He only knew that there was something about Madison's clear eyes, her flawless complexion and her shapely lips that did a number on his heart.

Still he hated to leave the woman right now in what she had to consider the house of horrors.

It would be like Brody having to live in the same apartment where Lindsey had...

He shook his head. He didn't want his thoughts to go there. He'd tried hard to put that behind him, even moved here to Virginia to get away from his old life.

But would he ever be able to truly put it behind him?

Yesterday had dredged up so many memories of Lindsey. There were so many similarities between the way he'd found Lindsey and the way he'd found Madison. The whole suicide scene brought back the remembrances. The only difference was that he'd shown up at Lindsey's place in response to a police call. He'd thought the address sounded familiar. But then he'd walked into her house and found her dead. He was still reeling from seeing her lifeless body when he'd found the suicide note.

I gave you my heart, and you walked away. Your arrogance has hurt too many people. You never consider other people's feelings...

He and Lindsey had met at one of Manhattan's trendy clubs and dated for three months. Lindsey, a teacher by trade, had been a nice girl, except when she drank—which had happened all the time. Brody had thought if she got some help that the two of them might have a chance at a relationship. But Lindsey wouldn't even acknowledge that she'd had a drinking problem. Brody had broken up with her, hoping that might be a wake-up call. Things hadn't ended the way he'd hoped. Not at all.

He shook the memories off. He needed to check with the other detective to see if he'd found out any new information about the other two suicides that had happened in York County since Brody had arrived. What if they weren't suicides, either? What if there really was a serial killer loose here in York County?

He strode over to Detective Blackston's desk as soon as he got to work. The detective, long and lean—a former cross-country runner—glanced up from some files on his desk.

"Find out anything yet?" Brody asked.

"I met with Willie's family this morning," said Blackston. "Both his mom and dad said they still had trouble believing he would have committed suicide, even with all of the problems he was having emotionally at the time. But there's also no evidence to indicate that it wasn't suicide. I'm looking over the crime-scene photos now."

What Madison had told him about the egg timer remained stuck in his head. It had been an integral part of the crime. Had the other victims heard that egg timer also? None of the detectives would have thought anything strange to see an egg timer in someone's home. That would be the next thing that Brody investigated. That might just be the evidence that tied all of the cases together.

Brody's cell phone buzzed. He looked at the number and saw that it was Madison. Immediately, he tensed. Had something else happened? He shouldn't have ever left her.

"Madison," he answered. "Is everything okay?"

"Everything's fine. Look, I was wondering if I could see the suicide note, Brody. Something about it keeps nagging me."

The suicide note? Now why would she want to

see that? "I can make you a copy. How about if I bring it to Kayla's place after work?"

"Perfect. Thank you."

Against his better judgment, he called to her before she hung up. "Madison?"

"Yes?"

"Are you sure you're okay?" he asked gruffly.

"Yeah, I'm fine, Brody. Thank you."

Why didn't he feel reassured then?

Madison couldn't stand being in her own house alone. But she couldn't bear the thought of going back to Kayla's house and staying there alone, either. So instead she collected everything she thought she might need—some clothes that she'd left in the laundry room, her camera, her appointment book—got in her SUV and started driving. The open road seemed safe enough.

But even on the open road she couldn't outrun her memories. The feeling of the noose around her neck, the needle being injected into her neck, the panic that had raced through her began to close in on her.

Just what the killer wanted, probably. Death was too easy. Once it was done, it was done. But for someone twisted, playing these mental games could really give them their kicks.

How had her would-be killer gotten her cell-phone number? Whoever had done this had planned in advance. He'd left the noose in her room, he'd sent her that stupid egg timer, he'd probably studied her to see when she came and went.

This wasn't a random act of violence. But why Madison? Why, of all the people in Seaford, had the killer picked her to torture? It just didn't make sense. Did he have some kind of connection to her?

She just had to trust that God was watching over her, and rely on her faith to get her through this. Her faith had been her only comfort in life's trying times. She knew it could sustain her now, too. It also helped to know that Brody was doing his job and would track down the madman. Trusting both God and Brody was all she could do. She wasn't one to play detective herself.

Except she did want to see that suicide note. Something had been bugging her. She wasn't sure what. But the killer had been specific about what she wrote. There had to be a reason for that.

She hadn't been able to reach the baseball coach over at the high school, so while she was out she decided to swing by there. Kids were on summer break right now, but she knew that Coach Daniel would be at the school. She needed to talk to him about rescheduling.

The school had been a big client for her and she didn't want to lose the business. Madison took all of the sports pictures for the school, as well as yearbook photos. Thankfully the baseball coach was someone Madison knew from church. Daniel only moved here eight months ago, but he, in some ways, seemed like the brother she never had. They had an easy, lighthearted friendship that Madison appreciated. The man was close to her age and was known for always wearing a baseball cap backward, she assumed to partially cover up his early hair loss.

Sweltering heat surrounded her when she emerged from her SUV. She hurried across the parking lot toward the baseball field. In the out-field Madison spotted members of the varsity team running through drills. She shielded her eyes from the sun and looked for Daniel. She knew he had a makeshift office beside the concession stand, so she decided to search for him there.

She stepped onto the concrete floor of the dimly lit building, bypassed the cabinets stocked with candy bars and chips and headed for the door on the far side of the room. Rock music blared from that direction. She tapped at the door, but heard no response.

"Daniel?" She pushed the door open slightly. A messy room filled with bats, balls and old uni-forms came into view.

As the door opened farther she spotted Daniel

seated in a ratty chair in the corner. He hadn't heard her, apparently. In his hand he held a needle, poised in the air.

Madison gasped and stumbled backward. Horrifying memories flashed through her. Daniel? Was Daniel her attacker? It didn't seem possible. But he did fit the description height-and-weight-wise.

"Madison?" He put the needle onto a nearby table and stared toward her. His eyebrows pivoted together. "What's wrong?"

She pointed to the needle. "You…? You…"

He looked back at the piece of medical equipment. "Do shots freak you out? I know some people hate needles. I've had a while to get used to them."

Madison blinked back confusion. What was he talking about?

"I'm diabetic. I thought you knew."

Diabetic? Daniel? She'd had no idea. She released an airy laugh.

Diabetic.

"I'm sorry, Daniel. I'm not laughing because of your diabetes. I'm laughing because of my foolish reaction. I'm so sorry."

"It's no problem. I was just giving myself a little insulin shot, and I didn't hear you come in." He looked at her more closely. "Is everything okay? You're not looking too hot."

She self-consciously touched the raw skin at her neck. Though she'd worn a high-neck shirt, she still felt like everyone could see her wound. "I'm okay."

He narrowed his eyes. "Why don't I believe you? It was unlike you to miss our appointment yesterday. Then you show up today with circles under your eyes, a busted lip and jumpier than a bean."

She swallowed…or tried to, at least. "It's nothing. Really. I'm fine."

He shifted. "Look, Madison, I don't want to pry, but did someone hurt you? You didn't start dating some guy who's bad news, did you?"

She shook her head. "No, it's nothing like that. I just…" How much should she share? Certainly gossip had already begun to spread all over town. That's what happened in small, close-knit communities like Seaford. She shrugged finally. "A man broke into my home yesterday and attacked me."

Daniel's eyes widened. He reached for Madison's arm in obvious concern. "Madison, I'm so sorry. Did they catch whomever did it?"

"Not yet. They're still working on it."

He stepped back and put his hands on his hips. "You've got to get Brody on the case. He used to work homicides up in New York City, you know.

If anyone could track down the person who did this to you, it's Brody."

Madison tilted her head in surprise. "You know Brody?"

"We work out at the same gym. I think all the women there plan their schedules at the times when Brody's usually there. He's quite the ladies' man, apparently."

Madison nodded, reeling from his proclamation about Brody being a womanizer. "Brody *is* on the case, and I wouldn't know anything about the ladies' man part. As far as I'm concerned, he's just the lead detective."

"Probably a smart idea. He's a nice enough guy, just not the family man type."

Madison had no interest in Brody, so why did Daniel's insinuation bother her? She wasn't looking for a family man—any man for the matter.

She nodded toward the field. "Can we reschedule the pictures for tomorrow?"

"Sure thing. I'll make sure my guys are ready."

"I appreciate it, Daniel." She started to walk away when Daniel called to her. She turned.

"I asked Kayla to dinner tonight."

Madison raised her brows. "Kayla? I had no idea you two were dating."

He shrugged. "I've wanted to ask her out for a while, especially seeing how you're not interested." He winked.

Madison waved him off, used to his jesting. "Such a charmer, you are."

His quick smile slipped. "Kayla said she was making dinner tonight and I could come over, but that you might be there."

"I can make myself scarce."

He laughed. "No, no. That's not what I was trying to imply. I'm just having a hard time getting a read on her. I can't tell if she's politely trying to blow me off."

"I'll tell you what. I'll see what I can find out—but only because I feel sorry for you."

He clutched his heart in mock pain. "Ouch. You reject me, then cut into me with that line?"

"Only because I know you can take it." She punched his arm lightheartedly. "In the meantime, I'll see you for dinner tonight."

"You're the best, Madison."

She shook her head with a grin.

The exhilaration of a new relationship. Now that was something that could distract her from the problems at hand…as long as she wasn't a part of the equation.

By the time Madison grabbed a milk shake from a fast-food restaurant and then stopped by the drug store for a few items, Kayla was already back at the house with Lincoln. Madison walked in and soaked in the scent of garlic and onions.

She only had a minute to enjoy it before Lincoln darted toward the front door and into her arms.

Her body still ached from yesterday, but she could ignore those pains as her son wrapped his little arms around her neck. "How was school today?"

"It was good. I want to go home now, though, Mommy." His little boy eyes pleaded with her.

"We're going to stay here for a few more days, okay? Our house got a little messed up, so we have to make sure it's all back in order before we go there."

"What happened?" He tilted his head innocently. Madison wanted nothing more than for him to hold on to that innocence for as long as possible.

"It's nothing for you to worry about it. We'll get everything back together. It won't be much longer...I promise."

"Madison!" Kayla appeared around the corner wearing a white apron splattered with marinara and a wooden spoon in hand. "I was just cooking dinner. Will you be staying here again tonight?"

"Is that all right?"

"More than all right. I'm happy to have you guys here. But if it's okay—"

"—Daniel is coming over to eat tonight." Madison finished for her.

Kayla's eyes widened. "How did you know?"

"I ran into him at the school. I'm doing a photography job for the baseball team. And, of course, that's fine."

Kayla blushed. "Okay, great. Dinner won't be anything exciting. I'm just hoping it's edible, for that matter."

Madison wanted to ask more questions, but didn't. She didn't quite know Kayla well enough to do so. Though Madison didn't want any romantic entanglement in her own life, she loved seeing budding romance in others. It was such an exciting time. She had her own sweet memories of being in love. It was a once-in-a-lifetime experience for her. "I'm sure whatever you're cooking will be great. It smells delicious."

"I'm actually glad you're both going to be here because I hate those awkward moments that can happen on first dates. I get so nervous!"

Madison smiled. "Maybe it won't be awkward. Maybe you'll both have plenty to talk about."

"Maybe. You probably dated plenty, didn't you?" Kayla asked. "I mean, you're gorgeous so I'm sure you have no shortage of men vying for a chance with you."

Madison shook her head. "Not really. Reid was my first love. We started dating in ninth grade. We dated on and off for the rest of high school and college and then we got married after we both graduated."

"Wow, that's incredible. I don't know too many people who ended up marrying their high-school sweetheart. That's a real accomplishment."

Madison smiled wistfully. "Yeah, it was."

Lincoln tugged at her shirt. "Mom, come see what I made in school today."

Madison excused herself and followed her son back to the guest bedroom so she could gush over his art projects. A few minutes later the doorbell rang, and Madison heard Daniel's booming voice from the front of the house. Madison and Lincoln joined the couple in the kitchen.

"Madison, good to see you again." He kissed her cheek. "The food smells wonderful."

Kayla blushed again, soaking in all of Daniel's attention. No sooner did a round of small talk begin than the door bell rang again. Before Kayla could stand, the door opened and Brody stepped inside.

"Please, join us to eat. We were just about to sit down," Kayla said, leading him into the kitchen.

Madison drew in a light breath when Brody came into the room. He just seemed to have that effect on people. Anyone could see he was easy on the eyes. He didn't seem to hold it over people, though. Still there was something about him that was so mysterious, that seemed impossible to get past.

Of course Madison wasn't supposed to get past

any walls that Brody had put up. She was merely an acquaintance. But why did the idea of getting to know him better seem so intriguing, then? She chided herself. She was getting into dangerous territory with her thoughts. She needed to keep her distance.

"Madison."

She nodded his way. "Brody."

Lincoln looked up at him. "You're our neighbor, the one that never talks to us."

Madison wanted to bury her face. "Lincoln!"

"No, it's okay." Brody chuckled. "I admit, I haven't been the best neighbor. I'm going to try and do better."

Lincoln's chin jutted out and he nodded, hands on his hips. "You can start doing better by playing baseball with me sometime."

"Lincoln!"

Brody chuckled again. "He's got spunk—I like that. I would love to play baseball with you sometime, Lincoln. I think it's a great idea."

"I always say if you want something you should go after it," Daniel said. "I think I'm looking at a future member of my baseball team right here."

Brody reached his hand out. "Good to see you, Daniel. It's been a while."

"Your fan club at the gym has been very disappointed by your absence lately."

"Fan club? That's the first I've heard of that."

Madison had to give him some points for at least appearing humble. She wondered if he secretly relished the attention, though.

"Won't you stay and eat, Brody?" Kayla asked. "We have plenty."

Madison watched as Brody squirmed for a moment. She could only imagine that he was trying to think of an excuse to leave, to get away from her. Apparently nothing came to mind because he said, "I guess I can stay for a few minutes. But I will have to eat and run, so don't be offended."

"I'm just happy that you're actually staying. I don't get to spend enough time with you, cousin. You're always too busy working."

Everyone made pleasant small talk as dinner began.

Halfway through, Brody looked at his watch. "Madison, could I steal a minute of your time before I run?"

"Absolutely."

Brody stood and placed his napkin on the table. "Kayla, the meal was wonderful. Thank you for having me over."

"Let's do it more often."

"I may have to take you up on that. Your cooking definitely beats the microwave meals I'm used to eating."

Madison cast another glance at Lincoln. He

was busy chatting with Kayla and Daniel. He'd gotten the gift of gab from his father and he used his gift as often as possible. Seeing how at ease he was with others brought her both pleasure and distress. One could never be too careful in the world.

Madison followed Brody into the living room. He pulled a piece of paper from his jacket pocket. "Here's a copy of that note I promised you."

She took the paper from him and, as she did so, her throat went dry. She wanted to see it, but she didn't. Instead of looking at the note, she folded it again and put the square in her jeans' pocket. "Thank you."

He didn't say anything for a moment. "Any reason why you wanted to see that?"

"Just something about it is bothering me. I want to read it again and see if I can figure out what." She shifted her weight. "Any updates on the investigation?"

"We're working as hard as we can, but nothing yet. The man left no prints, no hairs, no fibers, nothing."

"He was like a ghost."

"It's still early. Don't get discouraged."

"Discouraged probably isn't the right word. It's more like terrified. I don't like being afraid to be in my own house. I just don't know who to trust or how to protect my son." She attempted a weak smile. "As a certified control freak, this is really knocking me off-kilter."

Brody shifted. "What can I do, Madison?"

She shrugged. "Nothing, Brody. I'm sorry I vented. I don't expect anything from you. I just…" She blew the air from her lungs and looked into the distance. "I'm going to get back to dinner. Thanks for the note."

She slipped away before her emotions got the best of her.

SEVEN

Brody remained at the front door, his hand on the knob, as he contemplated staying or going—the same song and dance he'd gone through earlier when he'd left his neighbor. He wanted to keep his distance, to remain professional. But another part of him, a part that he thought he'd buried, wanted desperately to help her, to ease her fears, to carry her burden.

But, of course, he had to go. He had a job to do and that was the true way he could help Madison—by finding the would-be killer. The investigation was just moving much more slowly than he'd wanted and with every minute the culprit could be getting away.

That was unacceptable.

He wanted to go and talk to the families of the two other suicide victims also. He knew his colleagues had questioned them already and he didn't want to make them stir up any of those devastating memories again. But Brody just felt like there was something they were missing… much like Madison with that suicide note.

Right now, he'd go ask about the timers. That might be the best lead they had at the moment. He'd start with Victor's family. They'd claimed from the beginning that Victor wasn't the type to commit suicide, even if he had struggled with depression.

It was a shame, on more than one level, that Victor was no longer with the Sheriff's Department. Victor had been one of the first people to try and befriend Brody when he'd arrived at work the first day nearly a year ago. Then one morning in June Victor didn't report in to work. Another deputy had gone to his place and discovered his body. No one had seemed too surprised by the suicide note. Family members never wanted to believe that their loved one had committed suicide, though.

Brody hoped that Victor's mom wouldn't mind him showing up at the doorstep. He knocked tentatively, trying to gather every ounce of bedside manner that he had. A moment later Mrs. Hanson answered. Her eyes were red-rimmed, and Brody wondered if she was still mourning the loss of her son. She'd probably be mourning for the rest of her life. People never seemed to get over the deaths of their children.

"Detective, what can I do for you?" She sniffed and gripped the door handle like a lifeline.

"Ma'am, I was hoping I could ask you a few questions concerning the death of your son."

"Detective Blackston was just here earlier today."

"A few additional questions have come up," he explained gently.

She hesitated before nodding and stepping back to invite Brody inside. "Of course, I'll answer them. Especially if it means proving my son didn't commit suicide. He loved me too much to take his own life." She released a long, shuddering breath. "He was finally getting back on track. He loved his job with the Sheriff's Office. I've said from the beginning that something doesn't add up."

Brody sat in the armchair that Mrs. Hanson led him to. "I have one specific question for you, if you'll humor me. There's a key piece of evidence we might have missed, one that may have seemed insignificant at the time."

"What would that be?" She lowered herself onto the couch across from him.

"An egg timer."

Her eyebrows flicked up. "An egg timer? The kind you wind up? The old fashioned sort?"

"Yes, ma'am."

She nodded. "Of course, I have one. I have a

couple, actually. I use them all the time when I'm cooking my pies."

"Can I see them?"

"I'll grab them from the cabinet."

He glanced at the house, a clean, sparsely decorated space, as she disappeared into the kitchen. He tried not to tap his foot impatiently as he waited. He wanted answers and they seemed to be within his grasp. A moment later Victor's mom reappeared with two white timers in hand.

She held up one. "This is my old one, the one I always use." She held up a second one. "This one we got in the mail. It doesn't work very well, but I kept it as a backup."

"May I?" He reached for it.

"Of course."

He turned over the timer, his heart racing. This was the same timer that someone had mailed to Madison. There was no such company on the record in York County or the surrounding areas.

"Was there anything strange about this timer? Do you remember seeing it anywhere unusual after Victor's death? Think carefully because this is very important."

"I don't even have to think about it—I know the answer. I found this timer in the bathroom. I thought it was strange, but no one else did. I always keep my timers in the kitchen and Victor never used them for anything. He'd have no reason to have it in the bathroom. I thought maybe, just maybe, he'd used it so he wouldn't be late for work or something. I had no idea."

"This was a huge help, Mrs. Hanson. Do you mind if I take this with me?"

"If it will help to prove my Victor didn't commit suicide, then you can have it and anything else in this house, too. Just clear my boy's name."

"I'll do my best," he promised.

After Madison got Lincoln to sleep, she went into the dining room. She'd been so keenly aware of the note in her back pocket, that it seemed like the paper seared through her denim into her skin. Kayla had disappeared into her own bedroom, so Madison guessed she had a few minutes of privacy. She wanted to read this note again when she was sure she was alone so she'd have some time to process the words there.

She lowered herself onto a chair at the dining-room table, feeling like she was bracing herself for bad news. Her hands trembled as she pulled the paper from her pocket. She took several deep breaths before unfolding the note. With slow, steady movements Madison spread it smooth across the table. Before her eyes even focused on the words, she soaked in the handwriting. Usually she wrote with flowing loops. Reid had always said she had artistic handwriting that was as pretty to look at as her words were to read. The handwriting on this paper looked uneven. It told the tale of her distress while writing it.

She closed her eyes and whispered a prayer, knowing she'd need divine strength to relive the nightmare she was about to unveil. Slowly she pulled her eyes open and, ignoring her rapidly beating heart, looked at the words she'd scribbled.

By the time you read this, I'll be dead. Really, this whole event was a long time coming. On a brighter note, I love my family very much. One of the most precious things in life. Know I loved you, Lincoln. Love wasn't enough, though, to get me through my heartache after losing Reid. You're better off without me. No more pain for me.

Tears sprang to her eyes, but she tried to pull them back. She'd never leave Lincoln. Never. He was her whole world.

Her pain turned to anger that the man had forced her to write those words. If Brody hadn't found her before she'd died, then her son would always have thought that she'd abandoned him and taken her own life.

It was enough to make her want to track down her would-be killer herself and hand him over to the authorities. He'd even known enough about her that he'd included her son's name in the note. Her heart felt ice-cold at the thought.

Why had her attacker picked these words? What was so important about her writing these sentences exactly as he dictated? It just didn't make sense. The cadence of the words was off. Like on the sentence that started with "On a brighter note." Then the next sentence was just a fragment. If the killer had so carefully planned the note, why had he chosen those awkwardly phrased sentences?

She leaned back in the dining-room chair. What if the killer was trying to say something else through the note? She stared at the words a moment, trying to figure out if there was some code to the letters. What were some codes that people used? Every third letter maybe? She tried it, but only ended up with an odd assortment of letters.

After trying the first letter of every word and various other ideas, she felt ready to give up. She put her forehead to the table, fighting tears.

"I didn't know you were still up."

Madison gasped and jerked her head back. Kayla stood in the kitchen doorway. She relaxed slightly and chuckled at her overreaction. "Kayla."

Her friend approached the table, a sympathetic

expression on her face. "I didn't mean to scare you. I should have known better."

Madison waved her off, even though her heart still beat double time. "You're fine. I'm just looking at this note that the man forced me to write. Something's off about it and I'm trying to figure out what. It's got me on edge."

Kayla stepped forward. "You mind if I look? I'm pretty good with puzzles. Maybe I'll see something you didn't."

"Go right ahead."

Kayla sat beside her and cautiously took the paper, slipping it from Madison's hand. Her eyes scanned the words there for what felt like hours. "Maybe there's some kind of hidden message here. Is that what you're thinking?"

"That's exactly what I was wondering."

Kayla glanced up. "What have you tried already?"

Madison told her about all of the brainstorms she'd had, none of which had panned out.

Kayla narrowed her eyes at the paper. "How about the first letter of every sentence?"

Madison gripped her pen against the scrap paper in front of her. "Read them to me."

"B, r, o, o, k, l, y, n."

Madison stared at the paper. "Brooklyn? The letters spell *Brooklyn*. That can't be a coincidence, can it?"

"I don't think so." Kayla's face looked white. "Brody's from Brooklyn. I don't think that can be a coincidence, either. You need to call him. Now."

Twenty minutes later Brody showed up again at Kayla's house. Madison could see the worry and curiosity in his gaze as he stepped inside. She could also see the weariness in his eyes. He was operating primarily on caffeine, Madison would bet. Every minute that he wasn't watching over her, she could easily see him working on the case, even if it meant forfeiting sleep.

Brody turned to Madison. "What's going on?"

Madison held up the note, not wanting her heart to soften too much. What if Brody had more to do with this than he let on? The note had spelled the name of the place Brody had just moved from. What if he wasn't innocent in all of this? "I knew there was something strange about the words I had to write on this note, so Kayla and I decided to play detective. We discovered that the first letter of each sentence spells the word *Brooklyn*."

His eyes narrowed. "As in Brooklyn, New York?"

"Exactly."

He reached for the paper. "Can I see the note again?"

Madison handed it to him. He studied it for several minutes, grunting and nodding. A certain melancholy seemed to settle over him. "Good work, ladies. I'm going to look into this."

She wasn't going to let him leave that easily. "Brody, why would someone send a message to you through a supposed suicide note that he had me write?"

Something dark passed through his gaze. "I don't know."

Madison had the feeling there was more to the story than that. But what exactly did Brody know? What connection did he have to this case other than being the lead detective? "What aren't you telling us, Brody?"

A wall seemed to go up around him, and his voice turned to steel. "There's nothing that I'm not telling you."

"Nothing, Detective? I find that highly unlikely."

Something flashed in his eyes. What was it? Fear? Annoyance? "Let me draw the conclusions, Madison. Let me do my job."

"My life is the one on the line, Detective."

His gaze didn't break from hers, sending the clear message that he wouldn't back down. "There are parts of the case that I can't share with you, not until we have something firm nailed down."

Madison didn't say anything, but she felt sure

there was more to it. She'd find out eventually…
one way or another.

Because she wasn't going to let a madman get
away with this, and she didn't care who she had
to take down to make sure that happened—even
Brody.

Brody left his cousin's house, still feeling cold
at his core.

Brooklyn.

He had to look at those other suicide notes.

He'd already questioned the other families involved and gotten nowhere. All they'd said was
that they couldn't believe their loved ones had
committed suicide—but nearly every family in
this situation said that. He needed evidence, not
hunches.

And thanks to Madison's keen eye he may finally have what he needed to move this case from
attempted murder to serial killer.

He bypassed his coworkers at the sheriff's station and went straight to his office. The files for
the other two cases were already on his desk. He
opened them and rifled through the papers until
he found copies of the suicide notes.

His eyes scanned the words there, writing
down the first letter of each sentence. When he
was done, he sat back in his chair and stared at
the word in front of him.

Madison.

The killer had been targeting Madison before they'd even realized there was a killer.

He had a feeling he knew what the message in the next note was. He jotted it down just in case. He was right. The first word had been *Victor,* the name of the second victim.

So why had the killer changed course and made Madison write *Brooklyn?* Unless he wasn't telling them the name of Brody's old precinct, but of his next victim.

He had to talk to the sheriff.

It took forever for sleep to find Madison. She'd tossed and turned in bed, her mind racing with possibilities. What in the world was Brody hiding? And why? What was the reason for his aloofness?

All she knew for sure was that his secrets might be hindering the outcome of her case.

The man could get under her skin, but she'd always assumed he was on her side. Maybe her initial impressions of him were correct. Maybe he was simply rude, arrogant and completely self-centered. She could live with those things—or at least learn to ignore them. But if he was somehow involved in this case and not telling her about it...that was a different story. This was her life on the line.

Images began battering her again. She pictured the man hiding silently in her bathtub with his weapon drawn. She remembered the fear that had rippled through her as her shaky hand wrote the dictated suicide note. She felt the familiar jolt of paralyzing fear at the thought of dying and leaving Lincoln all alone.

In an instant life could be forever altered. She thought she'd already learned that lesson, but here it was slapping her in the face again. When would she learn to fully rely on her faith instead of constantly giving in to fear?

Lord. I'm sorry my trust in You is so quickly swayed by my anxious thoughts. You're my strength, my refuge and protector, and even through life's hurts, You've never let me down.

But when she fell asleep, the nightmares still came.

She couldn't wake up. Nor could she breathe. The scent of leather consumed her. Tension squeezed her chest. And the faceless man from her nightmare grabbed for her. As hard as she tried, she couldn't escape. Her limbs had frozen.

She had to wake. Had to wake up.

An unknown pressure weighed on her. A dream? Then why didn't it feel like a dream, but reality? She had to escape.

Finally she jerked her eyelids open.

She stared at a nightmare.

Her attacker stood over her, his gloved hand pressed against her mouth. He'd come back. This wasn't a dream, but cold, hard reality.

She thrashed, trying to get away. But the man had her pinned, trapped, unable to escape. She wanted to scream, but no sound would emerge.

Madison knew without a doubt that the man had come back to finish what he'd started. What did he have planned this time around? Terror gripped her at the very thought.

Lord, help me.

EIGHT

Brody shoved the keyboard back under the desk and ran a hand over his face. He needed another cup of coffee. "From everything I can tell from my own search and through talking to the County Manager, there's no one named Brooklyn in York County."

Sheriff Carl leaned over the desk, staring at Brody's computer screen. "Maybe the killer is operating outside of York County. Maybe he's targeting someone in one of the nearby towns. Or maybe we're just assuming Brooklyn is a person. Maybe the killer is taunting you."

"Why would he break his modus operandi now? Every letter has spelled out the name of the next victim. I think it's just a coincidence that Brooklyn happens to be the place I moved from. To take this case in any other direction would be a mistake, in my opinion."

Sheriff Carl sighed and lowered himself into the chair beside Brody's desk. "I agree. I just don't know what that something we're missing is. Not yet."

Brody stared at Madison's suicide note again, each word burned into his memory. "This guy is sick. And I don't think he's going to stop until we catch him. The key is, when are we going to catch him?"

Brody put the letter down and picked up a pencil, instead. He twirled the device between his fingers and stared off in the distance, mentally running through everything that had happened. The killer had laid that clue out there for them, dangled a hint about who his next victim was. So why did they feel powerless to stop the next crime from happening?

Sheriff Carl turned toward him, his eyes softening a moment. "How's Madison holding up?"

Madison's face flashed through his mind and Brody inadvertently smiled. "She seems to be doing surprisingly well, everything considered."

Sheriff Carl seemed to study Brody's expression a moment. "She's a special lady."

"You've known her awhile?" Brody leaned back, ready to let his mind wander to something else for a moment. Sometimes you needed to step back from the facts in order to process them. Maybe this conversation would help him to do just that.

"I knew the family before they moved to

Florida." The sheriff laced his fingers together across his belly and let out a pensive sigh. "She goes to church with me also. She's struggled since Reid died, but she always keeps her chin up and she always works hard. Plus, she's got a great heart. It doesn't matter if she needs money herself, she's always the first one to step up when another family is in need at church. She's one in a million."

Why did the thought of that make Brody's heart warm? No one could deny that Madison was special. It was even more reason he needed to stay away from her.

"Don't hurt her, Brody."

He cut a sharp glance at the sheriff. "I would never want to hurt her, Sheriff."

"I've heard about your track record with women. I don't want Madison to end up as your flavor of the month. She deserves better than that."

"It's not like that, Sheriff."

"Maybe it's not. But in case it is, I just wanted to make it clear that I didn't assign you this case so you could flirt with a pretty woman. I assigned you because I believe you're one of the best in the department and you have far more experience in homicides than the other detectives."

The last thing Brody wanted to do was to explain to his boss how not only had he been misunderstood but how any remnant of the man he'd once been was gone. Tragedies did that to a person. Instead, he shifted in his seat. "I don't play games with people's hearts, Sheriff. I promise you that. You can't always believe the rumors."

"I'm glad to hear that."

"Can we talk about something else?"

Sheriff Carl raised his eyebrows and nodded slowly. "Absolutely." He sighed and leaned forward, the weariness of the case dragging at his features again. "We need to figure out why the killer is picking his victims. There's got to be a reason behind it. But what do Willie, Victor and Madison have in common? That's what doesn't make sense."

"They're all locals. They grew up in this area."

"But is that enough of a connection?"

Brody tapped his finger on the desk. "That's the question."

His mind went to Madison again, as it often did. Why did such an amazing woman have to be the target of a killer? Not that anyone deserved to be a target. But the world just seemed like it would be a much dimmer place without her. She had a gentle spirit and heart full of love.

It was obvious from the clues this man was leaving that the killer was taunting them. He wanted to play games with them, to toy with them.

A sick feeling settled in Brody's gut. He didn't like this. He didn't like this one bit.

First thing in the morning he needed to talk to Madison again. So much for keeping his distance.

Madison's heart nearly pounded out of her chest. Cold sweat covered her.

What would her attacker do now? And when he finished with her, would he go after Lincoln? Kayla?

Lord, help us.

"You weren't supposed to survive, Madison, but superstar detective Brody Philips found you just in time. I figure you survived for a reason. Everything's for a reason, right? Well your reason is going to be to give Detective Philips a message for me. Tell him I'm not done. Tell him there will be more. And tell him everyone's blood is on his hands." He leaned closer. "If you scream before I leave, I'll bypass the front door and pay your son a visit, instead. Do you understand?"

Madison nodded, knowing terror was written all over her features. She'd do anything to protect Lincoln. Anything.

Slowly, the man slipped away. Out of her room. Almost like a phantom he was so quiet.

She listened, waiting breathlessly to hear which direction he would go. Fearful he would walk toward Lincoln's room. But he was so quiet. She could hardly hear anything. Wondered if she'd imagined him.

But her lips still felt numb from where he'd pressed his glove over her mouth.

He was no dream, but a real-life nightmare, instead.

She felt frozen where she was. She needed to get up, to call the police, yet her limbs wouldn't cooperate. She felt chained to the mattress.

Lincoln…what if he'd gotten Lincoln?

The mere thought caused adrenaline to surge through her. In one swift motion, she was out of bed and hurrying down the hall. She threw the door open to Lincoln's room, fully expecting to see the man there, leaning over her son's bed just as he'd done to hers.

Instead, all was still.

She tiptoed to her son's bed and sat on the edge of the mattress. A moment later she heard his even breathing. He was okay.

Tears of relief rushed to her eyes, and her heart slowed a bit.

But where had the man gone? Certainly, he'd left.

Still, fear nagged at her.

She reached onto the nightstand and grabbed the phone. She dialed the number she now knew by heart—Brody's number. He answered on the first ring.

"Kayla, what's going on? Is something wrong?"

"It's Madison. And yes, something's wrong. You need to get here now. My attacker came back for a visit and he left a message for you."

As soon as she hung up, she had the thought that maybe she should check on Kayla. She hated to leave Lincoln, though, but why wake him up and scare him if there was no reason to do so. She'd leave his door open. Kayla's room was right across the hall, so Madison could still hear Lincoln.

Reluctantly she left Lincoln's side. She crept across the hall, her eyes darting from side to side in search for her intruder. All appeared quiet.

She gently rapped on Kayla's door. The moments stretched by. Was her friend okay? Should Madison bust inside? What if her friend was hurt at this very moment and she was just standing there?

Just as Madison reached for the doorknob, the door opened. There stood Kayla, sleepy eyed, but okay. Relief again filled Madison.

"You're shaking," Kayla said.

"Kayla, he came back. Into your house."

"Who came back?"

"My attacker."

"He was in my house?" Kayla's head swung from left to right, as if looking for him.

"I just called Brody. I had to make sure you were okay, though."

Kayla reached forward and gave her a hug. "I'm glad he didn't hurt you again."

The adrenaline that had propelled Madison to check on Lincoln and Kayla began to fade and shock about what had happened caused her to tremble all over.

A rap at the door caused both of them to swing their heads toward the noise.

"It's me. Brody. Open up."

The two women walked arm in arm to the door. Kayla fumbled with the locks until the door finally opened. Brody stepped inside, soaking both of them in. "Is anyone hurt?"

"No, we're fine," Madison mumbled.

"Let me check the house. Where's Lincoln?"

"He's slept through all of this. He's still in his room. No need to freak him out if we don't have to."

"Why don't you go in his room and stay with him until I'm done?"

Madison didn't want to be anywhere else, not until she knew for sure that her attacker was gone. She slipped inside the dark room and listened again for the even sound of her son's breathing. There it was. So peaceful and unaware. For a moment, she felt jealous. What would it be like to be naive again? Had every naive part of her been stripped away in the past few years?

Brody's frame appeared in the doorway. "Everything's clear," he whispered. "Except I haven't checked this room yet."

Chills again raced up her spine. What if her attacker had been in the closet this entire time? "Please do."

Using a penlight, he quietly opened the closet and peered inside. He then checked under the bed. "You're safe."

But was she? Would she ever be?

Brody stepped closer and lowered his voice. His nearness made her throat go dry. "I need you to tell me exactly what happened."

She nodded and crossed her arms over her chest as she followed him into the living room. Kayla paced by the couch. Her head snapped up when they walked in, and fear shone in her big eyes. "How did this guy get into my place? I checked the back door, the windows. Everything is locked. I never even heard anything."

Brody eased his cousin into a side chair before backing up until he sat across from her. "We don't know how the suspect is getting in. It almost seems like he has to have a key."

Kayla shook her head. "My parents are the only other people who have a key to my place."

"We'll figure that one out in a minute. Right now, I need to hear what happened tonight."

Kayla stood, the lines on her face stretched with tension. "I'll fix some coffee. I need to do something to stay busy."

Madison sat on the opposite end of the couch from Brody, the tremors still racking her body. She sat on her hands, trying to control the shakes, but they didn't go away.

Brody's guarded gaze met Madison's. "Would a blanket help?"

She shook her head. Nothing would help, but she didn't say that aloud.

"Are you ready to talk about it?"

Her trembling intensified as she mentally reviewed what to say. The scent of leather, her temporary paralysis as she realized the man was atop her, the helpless feeling that overcame her when she realized she was at the man's mercy—again. She pulled her legs under her and wrapped her arms over her chest. A blanket did sound good on second thought. She yanked a throw from the back of the couch and tucked it around herself.

When she looked up, Brody still stared at her, compassion written in the depths of his stare. He didn't say anything, only waited patiently for her to begin. She licked her lips and cleared her throat as she tried to work up the courage to relive the events of the evening. When she finally spoke, her voice hardly sounded like her own. "I woke up and he was over me, his hand slapped against my mouth so I couldn't scream. He said that since I survived, he figured there was a reason for it. The reason was that I was supposed to be his messenger."

Brody's eyes narrowed. "His messenger?"

"His message is for you." She locked gazes with the detective across from her, carefully watching his reaction.

Brody tensed, the action so obvious that Madison saw his muscles tightened all the way from the ridges in his arms to his jaw. "He has a message for me? What was it?"

She licked her lips again. "He said that everyone's blood was on your hands."

"My hands?"

"That's what he said. He made it sound like there would be more. He said 'everyone's.' What does that mean?"

Brody shifted. Before he answered, his cell phone vibrated. He pulled the phone off and put it to his ear.

Madison watched carefully as Brody's face hardened. She braced herself for whatever news he was receiving. Had they caught her attacker? Did they have a new lead? She could hardly stand waiting for him to hang up. When he did finally close the phone, he stood. His eyes had a tortured look about them.

"What's going on?"

"They just found another body. It looks like the work of your attacker."

Madison closed her eyes and sucked in a sharp breath. She had a feeling this was far from over.

Evil had just invaded her peaceful little town.

NINE

The woman's lifeless body lay across the carpeted floor, blood gushing around her. She'd—or more likely, a killer—had cut her wrists. The room was bare except for the woman's body, a bookcase with a few random pictures and an egg timer.

The woman could have been Madison. The only difference was that Brody had found Madison before death had claimed her. This woman hadn't been so lucky.

"What's her name?" Brody asked grimly, pen and paper in hand.

The deputy who'd arrived first at the scene placed his hands on his hips and looked at the body again. "Brooklyn Davis."

Brody's heart rate quickened and he gave the deputy a sharp glance. "Brooklyn, you said?"

"She just moved here a couple of months ago."

That would explain her sparsely decorated apartment, Brody mused. The room was now crowded with the medical examiner, two members of the crime-scene unit and members of the Sheriff's Department.

"The apartment manager had to come and check for a plumbing problem. He found her. Someone is notifying her family down in Georgia now."

"Any idea why she moved to York County?" Brody asked.

"She works at the hospital as a nurse."

A nurse? Brody pivoted until he could see the woman's face. He sucked in a quick breath. This was the nurse he'd met while Madison was at the hospital, the flirtatious one who'd worked behind the counter.

The killer was taunting them. He'd even reached out to Madison a second time in order to make sure they were getting the message. But somehow Brody seemed to be in the middle of this and not because he was the lead detective on the case.

Could this have any connection to Lindsey?

He shook his head. No, that was crazy. It was his imagination making connections that weren't there. What possible connection could Lindsey have to all of this?

Yet everything seemed so similar.

Brody swallowed resolutely, trying to push down his emotions. "I need to see the suicide note."

The deputy, wearing gloves, brought it to him. Brody pulled on his own gloves to examine the note. Before he even read the words, he soaked in the first letter of each sentence.

"William," he muttered

Sheriff Carl stepped behind him and shook his head. "We've got a lot of Williams around here. Take your pick."

"What do we do? Warn all of them?" Brody raised his shoulders with the question, exasperated by the generic name.

"We need to figure out a way to narrow it down."

Brody stepped toward the sheriff and lowered his voice. "The killer came back and left Madison a message tonight. He told her that everyone's blood was on my hands."

Sheriff Carl's eyebrows shot up. "On your hands? Any idea what that means?"

Brody shook his head. "No clue."

The sheriff's gaze turned serious. "I want you to keep an eye on Madison. If he sent her one message, he might get brave enough to try again. I want you to be there if he does…and be there to keep her safe."

"We have a deputy patrolling the house."

"It's not enough. This madman got past that deputy tonight, didn't he? She needs someone with her at all times. Her father and I were best friends growing up. I have to watch out for everyone in this town, but I especially need to watch out for Madison. The girl's already been through so much."

Brody shifted his weight and tried to keep his voice even. "How am I supposed to investigate this case and keep an eye on her? Respectfully speaking, sir."

"Staying closer to her might just be the best way to catch this guy. He'll be back. And I want you to be there when he does."

Madison stepped out the front door in the morning to tell Kayla and Lincoln goodbye and was surprised to see Brody in his sheriff's sedan out front. How long had he been there? All night? Was everything okay?

She marched toward his car, not caring that she was still wearing a bathrobe over her pajamas or about the sloppy ponytail slung at the back of her head. She'd been awake all night with nothing to do but think. And the more she thought about everything that had happened, the more questions she had.

Brody saw her coming and rolled down the window before she reached him. His green eyes seemed to have a subdued sparkle to them, despite the circles forming underneath them. "Good morning."

"What are you doing here, Brody?"

He leaned his head to the side, the action appearing to be out of exhaustion. "Keeping an eye on you."

She put a hand on her hip. "You don't have to do that."

"Sheriff's orders."

She nodded. Of course. Brody wouldn't keep an eye on her of his own free will. But Sheriff Carl was the exact type of person who'd be so concerned over her safety that he'd assign someone to guard her. "I see. So you've been out here all night?"

"Pretty much."

She tugged at the door handle and, finding it unlocked, she climbed inside and looked Brody square in the eye. "I need you to be honest with me. My life and the life of my son are on the line here. I need to know what's going on."

Brody looked away and drew in a slow breath. His jaw flexed a couple of times before he looked back at her. "The sheriff gave me permission to speak with you about some elements of the case. You might find what I'm going to tell you hard to hear, though."

Madison drew in a long breath. "Okay."

"It's about the murder I investigated last night."

"What about it?" she asked anxiously.

"It was made to look like a suicide, Madison."

Madison's heart stammered a moment. "Who was she?"

"Her name was Brooklyn. She had just moved here from out of state."

Her pounding heart seemed to freeze a moment. Brooklyn hadn't been as fortunate as she had been. Madison didn't know why she'd been spared, but she was thankful. A nudge of guilt crept in also, but she pushed it aside.

"There's more," Brody said.

"What is it?"

"There were two other suicides in the county. We thought they were just that—suicides. But it's now become apparent that they were murders, also."

All the air drained from Madison's lungs. "We have a serial killer?"

"I'm afraid so."

Madison ran her hands over her face. "This is just crazy. I…I don't even know what to think."

"It's a lot to soak in."

"Why is he targeting you, Brody? Why did he say their blood was on your hands? What aren't you telling me?"

"I have no idea, Madison," he ground out. "Sometimes people are just sick. They don't have rhyme or reason for what they do. Sometimes they're on drugs, sometimes they have mental problems. Who knows?"

"What now?"

"Now we hope he makes a mistake and leaves some evidence that will help us track him down."

She looked up at him. "How'd he get into Kayla's house last night?"

"Just like at your place, there's no evidence of a forced entry. It seems like he must have had a key. Now how he got that key, we don't know. There was no evidence of forced entry at any of the victims' homes." He exhaled sharply. "In fact, if you hadn't survived, Madison, we may not have even realized that we had a killer on our hands."

"Did he leave another note this time?"

"He did," Brody confirmed.

"And?"

"This has got to stay here, between you and me." Brody shifted to face her better. "He left the name William. We checked with the County Manager and there have got to be at least forty Williams in York County. We're in the process of narrowing them down."

"I see."

He sighed and leaned back. "So you're stuck with me all day."

Madison wondered if what he really meant was "I'm stuck with you all day." She said nothing.

"What's on your schedule?"

Her schedule? It seemed like the last thing on her mind at the moment. What did she have lined up? "I've got three or four appointments. I've got to do some photo shoots. I'm two days behind already."

"Consider me your chauffeur, then."

"I feel like you're more of a babysitter." She frowned.

"Don't be ridiculous. Being near you will only help the investigation. There may be some clue we're missing that I'll pick up on by talking with you."

Madison still felt like she was being babysat, but she didn't argue. Deep inside, she'd feel better if Brody were nearby, anyway.

Maybe, in some kind of twisted way, he was an answer to her prayer.

"How's it going staying with Kayla?" Brody asked an hour later as they started down the road.

Madison shrugged. "It's going fine. I'm glad Kayla opened up her house—it was very kind of her."

"I'm kind of surprised you're not staying with another friend by now."

She glanced over at him. "What do you mean?"

"I mean, you certainly have friends around here yet you're choosing to stay with Kayla."

Madison shrugged. "It's complicated."

"Explain, then."

Did she have to? The man had put his life on the line for her. It seemed the least she could do was make conversation with him for the duration of the car ride. Besides, this seemed unusual for him. He usually seemed to prefer quiet. "I grew up around here so, sure, I have friends in the area. But so many of them were friends with Reid and me. When he died...I think his death just reminded them all of how fragile life was. It was inevitable that our relationships changed." She sighed. "They pulled away, I pulled away... I'm not sure which one exactly. Probably both. I just know that suddenly we weren't having dinner every Friday night together anymore. It just seemed easier that way."

"That must have been painful."

"In a way, yes, it was. But in another way, life got busy. Being a single mom is no small task. Every spare minute I have is either spent working or with Lincoln. I know I should probably try to be more balanced and make more time for me, but it just hasn't worked out that way. Friendships kind of got placed on the back burner."

"Lincoln seems like a really good kid."

Madison smiled when she thought about her son. "He is. He's like his father in so many ways.

He's got his outgoing, talkative nature and the same adventurous spirit. That boy keeps me on my toes."

"And he's got a great name. I like that…Lincoln."

Madison smiled again. "Rcid and I talked about naming all of our kids after former presidents. We figured we could have a Jefferson, a Jackson, a Carter." Her smile slipped. That dream would never become a reality.

"What if you'd had girls?"

"We talked about naming them after presidents' wives. However, no one would have picked up on our pattern, though. There was an Abigail, a Hannah, an Elizabeth, a Rachel." Madison's smile faded. "But all of that doesn't matter anymore."

"It sounds like you and your husband had something good together."

Madison looked down at her hands a moment. "We did. It was like losing a part of myself when he died. I never want to go through that again. Never."

"Maybe that's the real reason why you let go of your friendships."

Her head snapped toward him. "What do you mean?"

"Getting close to people requires risk. It sounds

like you don't want to risk any more than you have to."

"Interesting theory from someone who doesn't know me."

His eyes softened. "Sorry. I overstepped my bounds."

Madison released her breath, trying to relax instead of biting Brody's head off. Maybe he'd gotten too close to the truth. "No, it's okay. I get a little defensive sometimes. Everyone seems to have an opinion on how I should move on since Reid's death. I say that until you're in my shoes, you have no idea."

Silence fell for a minute.

"What about you? You ever been married?" The man was certainly handsome enough. He was the kind of man who turned heads wherever he went. Perhaps he wasn't the type to settle down, though.

"Nope, never married." He said nothing else.

"Oh, come on. You've got to divulge more than that. Especially since I practically just told you my life story…at least, the hardest part of my life story."

He shrugged, and Madison noticed a sort of tension about him. "There's not much to tell. I guess you could say that I made some mistakes in dating, and my choices led to a lot of hurt. I'm trying to do the right thing now. Doing that means not dating until I get my head on straight. And sometimes I don't ever feel like I'll get my head on straight."

"What does that mean, Brody? What kind of mistakes could you have possibly made?"

"People called me a player. I don't know if I deserved that title, but I do know that I enjoyed not being committed. And, as a result, I made some poor choices."

Madison nodded, deciding not to ask him any more questions. She had a feeling it had been a huge step for Brody to even have shared that much. Men like him didn't like admitting their weakness. Madison thought that when a man admitted his weakness, it made him seem even stronger, though.

It was, on the other hand, good to know that he had no interest in dating. That should make their time together a lot more relaxed. She hated the games that singles seemed to play with each other, especially as they got older. She hadn't wanted to be thrust into the world of being single again, and she didn't welcome it with open arms. No blind dates for her, no one fixing her up, no online dating. She just wanted to be single and happy.

She couldn't deny, however, that she did miss the companionship of being married, of having someone to share your life with. She missed having a man around to help take the trash out and to take the car into the shop. She missed having someone to appreciate special dinners that she worked on for an hour or to tell her on occasion that she looked nice.

"We're here."

Madison focused on her surroundings and saw they were at the high school. She snapped away from her thoughts and turned her attention back to her photography.

Brody raised his arm in a half stretch, the small car hindering anything bigger. "You mind if I go to the baseball field with you? I have to stretch my legs for a minute."

"Absolutely."

They walked silently through the heavy summer sun toward the baseball fields. Madison could see the players pitching balls to each other. Seeing it reminded her of the promise Brody had made to Lincoln—that they would play catch. She hoped that Brody planned on keeping his promise. Because the only thing Madison feared even more than getting hurt herself was having her son get hurt again.

TEN

Brody watched Madison as she knelt on the grass to snap some pictures of the baseball players. There was a lot more to the woman than he'd initially assumed. When he'd first met his neighbor, she'd seemed friendly enough, but most women he'd encountered who were as pretty as Madison were either overly confident or painfully insecure. Madison had neither of those traits. Instead, she was down-to-earth, honest and kind.

And Brody was attracted to her. As much as he tried to deny it, he was. The more he was around Madison, the more his attraction seemed to grow.

At least they'd both made it clear that they weren't interested in a relationship.

No, he didn't deserve to be in a relationship. He'd made a lot of mistakes in his partying days. He'd caused irreversible heartache. Though he'd been largely misunderstood, he'd still hurt a lot of people through his refusal to commit.

For a long time he'd blamed the women he'd

dated. After all, he'd said at the time, they'd been the ones who'd assumed the relationship was more than it was. But Brody should have been clear from the start about his intentions. If he couldn't see a future with someone, he didn't want to stay in a relationship with them.

"I heard about what happened last night."

Brody turned and saw Daniel appear beside him. News did travel fast in these small towns. The news media would catch wind of everything before long. Then the pressure on the Sheriff's Department would mount even more. The FBI might even be called in.

"It was a rough night."

"Kayla said someone broke in while they were at home. That takes some nerve to come back a second time. Makes me want to find whoever's doing this and give them a piece of my mind…to say the least."

"That's for sure."

Brody's gaze scanned their surroundings, as he often did, looking for anyone who was out of place. Everything appeared peaceful and normal. The baseball team grinned for photos in between punching each other and putting rabbit ears behind their teammates' heads.

Daniel stared in the same direction. "Madison's a nice girl. A great photographer."

"I haven't seen her pictures yet, but I hope to one day."

"You should get her to show you. She's an ace with the camera. She can capture emotions that most people miss." His tone filled with admiration. "She's kind of like that as a person, too, you know? It's like she can see who people really are."

"I didn't realize you knew each other that well."

"We go to church together. We've hung out a few times otherwise."

Brody nodded. Had Madison dated Daniel? Madison had said she had no interest in dating. But the way Daniel had said "hung out" implied more. A moment of—what was that emotion— jealousy?—shot through Brody. It didn't matter if Madison had ever dated Daniel or not. She was free to do whatever she wanted. Besides, Daniel was a nice enough guy.

"Are you two...?" The way Daniel waggled his eyebrows made it clear he meant to ask "Are you two together?"

Brody shook his head. "I'm just doing my job, and right now my job includes watching out for Madison."

Daniel nodded slowly. "Sorry. I should have known better. Kayla told me you weren't the type to commit, anyway. You like to keep your options open."

Brody assumed the man was just trying to

make small talk to get on his good side since
Daniel obviously wanted to date Brody's cousin.
He was never a big fan of small talk, however.
"I'm not the type who likes to lead women on."
He'd have to have a talk with Kayla. He could
only imagine what his cousin had told Madison
about him. No wonder she acted so distant. Not
that Brody wanted her to act otherwise.

Madison appeared with her camera in hand a
moment later. She wiped at the mixture of dirt
and grass stains at her knees. Sweat glistened on
her forehead, thanks to the August heat. But she
still grinned, as if she didn't mind. "I think I'm
all done. I'll have these pictures back to you in a
week. Does that work?"

Daniel smiled. "Perfect." He extended his hand
to her. "Thanks for coming out."

Brody resisted the urge to slip his hand onto
Madison's back as they walked away. Daniel's
words still bothered him. Brody wasn't a player.
He'd just never met the right person for him.

He glanced briefly at Madison.

And he wouldn't even fool himself into thinking she was the right person. At least not until he
became the right person. But that would require
first paying for his mistakes.

Inside Brody's car Madison lowered her camera
and looked at the detective. He had the oddest

expression on his face, one that she couldn't read. Perhaps he was annoyed again? That seemed to be a common emotion for him. She didn't want to spend the energy trying to figure his mood out, though. She had enough other things to figure out first.

She cleared her throat. "I've got about thirty minutes until my next appointment."

He slipped his seat belt on. "You mind if we make a quick stop on the way there?"

"Sure thing, chauffeur." She leaned back into her seat. "Where are we going?"

"The grocery store."

"You need to do some shopping?"

"No, I'm trying to figure out where the killer got these egg timers. If we can track them down, then maybe we'll be one step closer to finding the culprit."

"Don't you think there's a better chance he got them online? Would he be that brazen to actually buy them here in town?"

Brody shrugged. "He's playing with us, so he just might be. Everyone slips up sometime. Everyone. This guy is no different. Somewhere he's left some evidence. He's left a clue that he didn't mean to leave. We'll find it, given time."

They pulled into the hometown grocery store. Bigger stores were located off the main highway through York County, but people often stopped by Alfred's Place for last-minute needs. Madison rarely did, especially since those last-minute "needs" for most people seemed to be alcohol or cigarettes. They were the main items advertised on signs and posters in the windows.

Madison stayed at Brody's side as they entered the store. Like any true small-town grocer, this was a place where patrons could buy motor oil, bug spray or fresh pastries, all on the same shelf. The place usually had locals outside gabbing in the gravel parking lot or groups of workers from the local seafood plant gathered around the coffee pot inside, wasting time until their shifts started.

A bell jangled as they stepped onto the stained linoleum floor of the place. The owner, Alfred Adams, looked up from sweeping in front of the check-out counter. The fifty-something-year-old man had a graying goatee, olive complexion and tattoos running up and down his arms.

"Afternoon," he mumbled. "Hot day out there, ain't it?"

"Without any breeze it is." Brody stepped toward him. "I'm looking for an egg timer. The white ones that you twist. Do you sell those here?"

"Sure do. Look down that aisle over there with the car air fresheners. I should have at least two." He nodded across the store, directing them to the corner at the back.

Brody and Madison exchanged glances as they started that way. She reached the timers first, gravitating toward them on the shelf. Madison handed one to Brody before picking up one herself. She examined it a moment, picturing the ad that had come with it. Don't Let Time Run Out on Our Special—it had seemed like a clever little advertising slogan. Instead, it had been part of a killer's long thought-out plot.

She looked up at Brody. "From what I remember, it looks like the same kind."

Brody turned it over and looked at the manufacturer. "It's the same brand." He gripped the device and walked back to Alfred. "You been selling these for a while?"

The man thought about it a moment before shrugging. "For as long as I can remember. Why do you ask?"

"Do you remember anyone coming in here in the past six or seven months and purchasing multiple timers?"

The man was quiet again before shrugging. "Not that I can remember. Not the kind of thing I think about. Course, I'm not the only one who works the counters in here. Someone else could have sold some. I usually only keep three in stock, though."

"Do you have any way of tracing who you've sold these to?"

Alfred snorted and shook his head. "Son, I'm what you young folks call 'old school.' I don't keep records like some of these new stores. If I see something's getting low, I order more. That's about it when it comes to inventory for me."

Madison's hopes plunged. This could have been the lead they were looking for. Now it appeared they were no closer than before.

"Is everything okay, detective?"

"We're trying to track down some leads in an investigation. If you can remember anything about those timers, I need to know."

Alfred paused from sweeping, his eyes at once curious. "I heard we had a serial killer on the loose. Are these timers connected?"

Brody stiffened. "A serial killer? Where did you hear that?"

"On the news this afternoon. Lead story. I never thought about locking my doors before. You better believe I will be tonight, though."

Madison felt her face drain of its color. She prayed that Brody wouldn't draw any attention to her, to give Alfred any clue that she was one of the intended victims. The last thing she wanted was to answer everyone's questions.

Brody scowled and pulled a card from his pocket. "If you think of anything, give me a call."

"Will do."

Brody put his hand on Madison's back to guide her out of the store. He led her to his car, and she glanced at her watch. They had just enough time to make it to her next appointment.

Just as they pulled away from the grocery store, an explosion shook the car. Madison turned around and saw the grocery store was in flames.

Madison gasped as she watched the flames that engulfed the old grocery store. The whole place was lit with fire. There was no way Alfred had survived. Even by the time Madison and Brody had arrived back on the scene, flames had licked every inch of the old wooden building. Three fire trucks surrounded it now and their hoses doused the fire. Numerous other safety vehicles surrounded the place.

Madison pulled her lips into a tight line. Poor Alfred. Though she hadn't known the man, she did know that no one deserved to die like this. They'd arrived too late to help the business owner. She did take some comfort in knowing that no one else had been inside.

Brody had ordered her to stay in the car. She could see him talking to Sheriff Carl in the distance. Sweat beaded on his forehead, partly from the heat of the day and partly from the inferno in front of him. From the way the two men talked, it seemed obvious that Brody was giving the sheriff a rundown on what he knew.

Sirens wailed in the background, signaling that more rescue vehicles were on their way. She shivered. Had the killer known they were going to be here?

Was he watching them now?

A few minutes later, Brody slid back into the driver's seat. Since he didn't reach for the steering wheel, it was obvious he didn't have intentions of leaving at the moment. He simply sat there, his head resting on the seat, the AC blowing on his face. After a couple of minutes he finally looked at Madison. "You okay?"

"You ask that a lot."

"You've been through a lot."

"I can't argue that. I'm fine, I guess. I just don't understand. Was that explosion intended for us? Was the killer laying in wait until we left and then he blew up the building? Or this is not connected at all, just a terrible coincidence?"

"We don't know the exact cause of the fire yet, but right now everything points to the propane tanks behind the building. An investigator will determine whether it was an accident or not."

"The tanks were behind the building? Someone could have been outside and caused the explosion."

"Or it could have just been a horrible chance event."

"There are too many coincidences. This wasn't an accident."

Brody's gaze fixated on her a moment, his eyes

serious and something unsaid playing there. "I think you're right."

"Could the killer have been outside the whole time?"

"It's doubtful. We'll know more later."

Madison shuddered. Was the killer lurking in the shadows right now? Was he always one step ahead of them and were they naive enough not to know it? Madison might be that oblivious, but not Brody. Certainly he would know. This killer just seemed so thorough, like he didn't miss a beat. How did he do it?

Brody squeezed her knee briefly, the action making her shudders become a shiver of awareness. "I need to go to the station for a minute. I need you to come with me."

She blinked at his words. "You need me to come with you?"

"I'm not letting you out of my sight. I'll pay you the money you're losing from forfeiting this photo shoot if I have to."

"No, I understand. I'll call and see if I can reschedule." Right now she had to think about the greater good. The greater good—more important than paying her bills even—was getting this man behind bars.

Madison's questions were excellent, Brody mused as he headed back to the station. Was the explosion meant to injure Brody or Madison? Had the killer been nearby, following their footsteps to the extent that he'd known they were going to that grocery store? But how would he have known? Even if the killer had had a suspicion, he wouldn't have known when Brody and Madison would have arrived. Certainly the man hadn't waited all day for them to show up.

Whoever this killer was, he was deeply disturbed. He needed to be locked up.

"Brody?" Madison's sweet voice broke him from his thoughts.

He pulled his gaze from the road for a moment to glance at her. "Yes?"

"Did you figure out who William is?" Her voice cracked as she asked the question.

"Not yet."

"What do you even do with that kind of information? Do you warn all the Williams in York County that they may be a serial killer's next target?"

"That would only cause chaos. We're looking into each of the people in the area who have that name. We're looking into their backgrounds, trying to figure out who might be the next target. The problem is that this killer seems to have no modus operandi. None of the victims have a lot in common." He sighed heavily. "The first two were men in their twenties—one single and one going through a divorce. Then our suspect targeted you, a widow and single mom. Next he targeted a single nurse who just moved to the area."

"We've all got to have something in common."

"I agree. We just have to figure out what."

Madison shook her head and leaned back into her seat. "We've got a serial killer here in York County. I never thought those words would leave my mouth. York County is such a safe place."

He gripped the steering wheel. "It *was* such a safe place. No place is immune to crime anymore."

"You have to admit you didn't even expect it here though, did you? You're from New York. You probably moved here to get away from all of that."

So much for that plan. Apparently, crime had followed him here. "I do like the slower pace."

Her voice changed from pensive to inquisitive. "Why'd you move here, Brody?"

The familiar ache between his shoulders returned. He prayed for a phone call or his gaslight to flicker on—anything to help him avoid Madison's question. Finally he realized he had no excuses. It didn't matter, he told himself. Neither of them were interested in a relationship, so there was no pressure to impress her. He shouldn't care what she thought. "I needed to get away. I needed to leave my old life behind."

"Was your old life that bad?" Her voice sounded quiet.

He shrugged and flipped up the AC another notch. "Depends on who you ask."

"I'm asking you."

He shrugged again and forced himself not to tug at his collar like he wanted. "I was living for myself."

"Doesn't bring you much pleasure, does it?"

"No, it doesn't." He glanced at her, happy for the excuse to change the subject. "You sound like you know."

"I had my moments in college of being totally self-absorbed."

He had a hard time seeing Madison as self-absorbed. "You don't seem like the type."

"Getting married and having a child helps you grow up. So does learning to rely on God."

God. That was one subject he hadn't expected to come up. "I wouldn't know about that."

"Not a churchgoer?"

"Not since I was a kid and then it was only on holidays. Am I allowed to call them holidays? Or do I have to say Christmas?"

Madison smiled. "Christmas, please. But don't change the subject."

He cut a glance at her and offered a teasing

grin. "You're not going to try and convert me, are you?"

"Am I trying to convert you if I say that it's too bad you've never learned to rely on God? It's never too late, you know."

"Yeah, I know. If I ever consider it, I'll let you know." He didn't ever plan on reconsidering, however.

"Relying on Him has helped me get through some dark days."

He hated to think about Madison going through dark days, but that was exactly what she was going through right now. If it was within his power, he'd scare away the storm clouds and make sure they never came back. "I've heard God's good for that."

"Give Him a shot sometime."

He looked over and smiled, not a wide, bright smile, but a mischievous one. "You're a little pushy sometimes. Did you know that?"

"I haven't been told that in a very long time, detective."

Why did hearing her say that bring him a certain amount of pleasure? Then he realized it was because they were flirting, one of his favorite pastimes. He needed to nip their playfulness in the bud before he got other ideas in his head. Madison was off-limits. Relationships were off-limits. He had to get his life figured out first.

ELEVEN

Madison's eyes scanned the pictures on Brody's office desk. The photos jutted out from a file folder, and she was pretty sure she wasn't supposed to see them since she wasn't a part of the investigation. The edges of the pictures teased her, though. She knew exactly what they were—crime-scene photos. Her gaze fixated on them.

A knot formed in her gut as the crime scenes came into focus. Horrific was the only word she could think of to describe the photos taken where lives had ended. It could have been her in those images. She would never take for granted how fortunate she was to have survived.

While Brody chatted with another detective in the other room, she picked up a photo. There was no body in this picture, but instead the photo captured other elements of the scene. Razor blades. An egg timer. Blood. All the pictures were taken in what appeared to be an otherwise empty room.

Madison picked up another picture and squinted

as she looked at it. This one was taken of the floor and showed a solitary shoe. In the background was a bookshelf. What about that bookshelf looked strange? There was something there that bugged her.

She looked closer and sucked in a breath. It couldn't be—but it was.

She put the photo down and leaned back in her chair, letting what she'd just seen sink in. She hadn't been seeing things or making anything up. Her eyes hadn't been deceiving her—had they? She picked up the photo again and looked at the small image in the background. Yep, it was there. She had to get Brody.

The framed image on the bookcase at this crime scene was one of her pictures.

That couldn't be a coincidence.

Shudders rippled down her spine as she hurried down the hall. The two detectives who were chatting stopped midsentence and turned to look at her.

She fumbled for words, wishing she'd sorted out how she'd bring up the conversation beforehand, especially since part of what she had to say meant owning up to her snooping. She held up a picture. "I shouldn't have been looking at this, I know. But I did. And I'm glad I did."

Brody stepped toward her, a knot between his

eyebrows. He reached for the photo. "What are you talking about, Madison?"

"This crime-scene photo," she held it up. "There's a framed photograph that I took in the background of this picture."

The detectives looked at each other, before Brody squinted at the crime scene photo. "The one of the Chesapeake Bay? How can you be sure? There are lots of pictures of the bay out there."

"I'm sure. I remember taking it. I remember that boat and that sunset. A photographer doesn't forget her own pictures. I took it."

Brody and the other detective looked at each other another moment before Brody finally nodded. "Let's look at those other crime scenes."

Madison sat on the couch at Kayla's house and flipped on the TV. She'd assured Brody that she'd stay put and keep all the doors locked until he returned. She knew the detective had to investigate the pictures from the crime-scene photos, on top of the explosion at the local grocer. In the meantime, a deputy sat outside her home.

Kayla was cutting out some shapes for the preschool class and Lincoln busied himself for a few minutes with some building blocks. Madison was thankful because she needed some time to decompress and process everything that had happened today.

A story on the news caught her attention. "A string of suicides in York County might actually be the work of a serial killer. So far three people have died because of a killer that many are calling the Suicide Bandit, who murders his victims but makes it looks like they took their own lives. The latest victim was found last night in the Dandy area in York County. Her name has not yet been released, but it's believed she was a nurse at a local hospital. One of the victims survived but has yet to be named by the police."

The video footage cut to a local reporter who stood at one of the piers in Seaford. Before Madison could listen to what the reporter said, a knock sounded at the front door. The ever-present tension in her shoulders tightened.

Kayla hurried into the living room and glanced uncertainly at Madison and then at the front door. "Should we answer?"

Madison stood, her reflexes on full alert. "Let's see who it is. Brody shouldn't be back yet."

Kayla tiptoed to the front door and peered through the peephole. "It's a man," she whispered. "I don't recognize him, but the deputy is with him."

The man knocked again, this time faster, more urgent. Since when did the Suicide Bandit knock?

Never that Madison knew of. Still, she wanted to be safe.

Madison crept forward and gazed out the peephole also. Some of the tension was released from her shoulders at the familiar face distorted on the other side of the glass. "It's Mark Zeskinski. He's a reporter for the paper." Madison unlocked the door and twisted the knob, careful to remain on guard.

"This man said he knows you and needs to speak with you," the deputy said.

"He's fine. I know him from work."

The deputy nodded and sauntered back to his vehicle. Mark cocked an eyebrow. A smirk teased at the corner of his lips. He'd always thought himself to be more handsome and charming that he actually was, and that was obvious now by the overwhelming confidence exuding from him as he leaned forward.

"Police protection?"

Madison shrugged. "Long story."

"You're a very hard woman to find, Madison."

"How'd you manage it?" The two had worked together on numerous stories where Mark had written the articles, and Madison had taken the pictures. Madison had always suspected that Mark liked her as more than a colleague, but as he stood here now, she knew his intentions were anything but romantic. His eyes were full of hunger—for a story.

"I'm a reporter. It's my job to track down people." He waited a moment before shifting his stance and looking beyond her at Kayla. "Aren't you going to invite me in?"

Madison shook her head and kept her arm across the doorway in an effort to not appear inviting. "No, I'm not. What are you doing here?" She stood in place to quickly shut the door and lock it, if necessary.

"You know what I'm doing here, Madison."

She forced her expression to remain neutral. "I'm afraid I don't."

His shoulders fell and he tilted his head in a chummy sort of way. "Come on, Madison. Give me my big break. Give me a jump on the broadcast media. You were one of the Suicide Bandit's victims, weren't you?"

Indignation rushed through her and her grip on the door tightened. "You shouldn't be here, Mark. Besides, I thought we were friends."

"We are friends. That's why you should give me the inside scoop here."

"Mark, what if I was the victim? And I'm not saying I am. But if I was the victim and I was your friend, I'd think you'd be more concerned about me than a story or a big break."

His eyes lost some of their cockiness. "I am

concerned. But—but you seem fine, so I didn't even think to ask how you were doing. I know you're a tough lady. And you obviously survived, so you must be doing pretty well. It could have been worse."

Madison didn't buy it. "I don't have anything to say to you, Mark."

She started to shut the door when his hand shot out. His shoulders slumped some and his eyes changed to pleading. "Come on, Madison. Please. This is the biggest story here in York County since the Colonial Parkway murders. A serial killer. In York County. It's all people are talking about."

"I'm sorry that I don't see it as glamorously as you do."

His gaze traveled down to where her shirt met her throat. "You were his victim, weren't you? I see the evidence on your neck."

Madison's hand shot to her throat. She'd forgotten about the burn marks there. Her shock turned to anger. "It's nobody's business. Leave me alone, Mark."

Before he could say anything else, Madison shut the door. She'd always considered Mark someone she could trust. Apparently he put his career before their friendship, though.

Her mind flashed back to those pictures she'd spotted in the crime-scene photos. She remembered a time when she'd downloaded all the pictures on her camera to Mark's computer so she could send them to their editor in time. He would have had access to those pictures.

She pictured the photos at the crime scenes. Were those some of the photos she'd downloaded to Mark's computer? She wasn't one-hundred percent certain, but she knew it was a good possibility. Plus, he knew her schedule. He could have figured out where she kept her spare key. He'd asked her out once and she'd said no, so perhaps he even had motive?

What if Mark was secretly the Suicide Bandit?

Her pulse raced at the possibility.

While Detective Blackston combed Alfred's house for clues, Brody decided to visit the other victims' homes once more. He wanted to look at those images that Madison had spotted in the crime-scene photos. Could she have been a target in this from the beginning?

The first home he visited was Victor's. The young man's mom answered again. Her eyes widened when she saw Brody. "Did you find out something new?"

"I was actually hoping to ask you another question."

"Of course."

He held up the crime-scene photo. "Do you

recognize the picture in the background of this scene?"

She studied it. "No, I don't remember seeing that before. I didn't keep tabs on my son, though. He was grown, so I didn't ask him about every picture he had in his room. Why do you ask?"

"The photographer who took these snapshots has pictures that showed up at every crime scene."

"So he's the murderer? The person who took these pictures is the Suicide Bandit?"

Brody raised a brow. "The Suicide Bandit?"

"That's what they're calling him on the news."

Great, the media had gotten ahold of this story. Things were about to get even more fun now. "No, the person who took these pictures isn't behind the crimes. In fact, she's one of the killer's victims. Only she survived."

Victor's mom gasped. "What a horrific experience she must have gone through. I can't imagine. Do you have any persons of interest in the investigation yet?"

"No, ma'am. Not yet. But we're working on this around the clock. I assure you that we're nowhere close to giving up on this investigation."

"I don't know that I'm going to be able to sleep at night anymore. Not knowing that this man is out there."

"I understand your concern. Lock your doors.

And thanks for your help. I know this isn't easy for you."

The woman reached for his arm before he could turn to leave. "Brody, find my son's killer. You're a kind man. I can see it in your eyes. Don't let this man get away with killing my son."

"I won't."

Victor had been a good man. A little naive and prone to drama, like many young people were. Brody remembered Victor's wife of only a few months had left him and sent the man's emotions into a tailspin just before his death. But Victor still had so much to live for. Just like that, life could slip through your fingers.

He thought about what Madison had said about God. He hadn't given much thought to God in years. He'd been too busy living for himself to think about anything else or any greater purpose.

How would his life have turned out differently if he'd been a believer? Madison certainly found a measure of comfort in her faith during this trying time. He could still see the peace in her eyes and he admired her for that.

But God wasn't for him. He'd lived long enough and seen too much to believe in a higher power.

He put his car into drive.

For some reason, that final thought rested heavy on his shoulders. But it lay even heavier on his heart.

* * *

The next morning Brody woke up from a rest-
less night of sleeping on the couch at Kayla's
house. He'd barely gotten any sleep, but he'd trade
that for a little peace of mind in knowing that
Madison was okay.

She had told him last night when he'd arrived
at Kayla's about the reporter who'd shown up at
her door. Anger surged through him at the nerve
of the man. It was a good thing Brody hadn't been
there. He would have definitely given the man a
piece of his mind.

But more than that, he thought about what
Madison had said about Mark having access to
her photos. The killer had to have gotten ahold
of Madison's work somehow. Brody had assumed
that the photos had been published somewhere
and that's how the killer had gotten them. But
Madison said these were all nature photos that
she'd never sold, that she'd taken for personal
pleasure.

The web became even more tangled.

Finally the rest of the gang at the house woke
up and saved Brody from his ever-churning
thoughts. Kayla whisked Lincoln off to preschool
and Madison didn't even have to ask about their
schedule for the day. She'd dressed prepared to go
to work with Brody again today, to abandon her

life until this guy was caught. They barely spoke until they reached the station.

"You're quiet," Madison said as she perched in the chair across from his desk there.

"Just thinking."

"About the Suicide Bandit?"

His eyebrow twitched up. "You watched the news, too, I assume?"

She nodded while frowning. "Yeah, talk about sensationalism."

"More like fear mongers." He shook his head. "People may have a right to know, but now we have everyone in town terrified."

"Maybe they should be scared. Fear keeps people sharp. Maybe now that people are aware, someone will see something or remember something."

"I talked to Detective Blackston last night and he said they'd gotten more than one-hundred calls ever since the story aired. Most of them are useless. People with good intentions, but faulty memories. I just hope chaos doesn't break out."

They stopped their conversation as Sheriff Carl approached Brody at his desk. He squeezed Madison's arm in greeting before his serious eyes fell on Brody. "Found out what caused the explosion yesterday at Alfred's."

"And?"

"A tampered gas line. Someone installed an

illegal line to the gas meter at the building and allowed natural gas from a street line to enter the air at an excessively high pressure," Sheriff Carl said. "When they did that, the gas line bypassed the meter's shutoff valve and its regulator. That's what caused the explosion."

Brody shifted his stance. "So was Alfred trying to steal gas or did someone else orchestrate all of that just to make the grocery store explode?"

"By all appearances, Alfred was up to some illegal operations," the sheriff said. "There have been rumors around here for months that he was selling that new drug Spice behind the counter and that he's had some involvement with illegal gambling operations. It looks like he probably ran that line himself."

"It just happened to explode five minutes after we left?" Madison asked.

"I know the timing seems crazy, but that is what appears to have happened. We're still investigating, though. There could have been foul play involved." Sheriff Carl leaned against Brody's desk and crossed his arms. "Here's the more important part, though. I sent a team to Alfred's house this morning, as soon as we got a search warrant."

"And?"

"We found everything there. Drafts of the suicide letters, leather gloves, syringes, the same rope used to make the noose, razors, drugs. Everything. It looks like Alfred was our man, that he was the Suicide Bandit."

Brody's heart rate didn't slow for some reason. "Alfred was the Suicide Bandit?"

Sheriff Carl nodded. "That's what the evidence says. We did a background check on him. It turns out he's done time for assault and battery. A former girlfriend filed the charges somewhere around ten years ago. His mama committed suicide, also. Overdosed. Still, it gives him a possible motive." He scrubbed a hand across his jaw. "We've got means. Now we're just trying to account for his time during the murders to make sure he had opportunity."

"He fits the size of the person who attacked me," Madison muttered.

Sheriff Carl nodded. "It seems like a slam-dunk case."

Brody narrowed his eyes. "Almost too much of a slam dunk."

The sheriff shrugged. "We just have to trust the evidence—and the evidence makes Adams look guilty right now. I'm looking forward to telling the fine people of York County that they can finally live without fear."

But could they, Brody wondered? Could they really?

Madison watched the sheriff walk away and shook her head. She should be grateful that the killer had finally been discovered. Instead, she felt even more concerned. Perhaps her heightened emotions wreaked havoc on her logic? Or was it her gut trying to tell her something else?

Brody turned toward her. She tried to read the expression in his eyes. Wariness? Or relief? "I guess it's like the sheriff said. You can finally sleep at night."

She nodded slowly, uncertainly. "I guess I can."

Silence fell for a moment. Madison didn't know what to say. So much of her and Brody's conversations had revolved around finding this killer. Both seemed to be in shock over the news about Alfred. Of all the things that Madison expected to discover after the grocery store explosion, finding out that Alfred was behind the crimes was the least of them. Now that she thought about it, she did get her house key made at his place. He could have somehow gotten a copy of her key that way. Still, everything felt surreal.

Brody stood, glancing around at the scurry of activity occurring at the station. He looked back down at Madison. "How about if I drive you back to Kayla's? No need for you to be here while we comb through everything."

She nodded again. "Of course." She could have directed him to take her to her actual home, but she didn't. Why did fear still course through her at the thought of being home alone? She had nothing to worry about anymore. It would take time to reprogram her thoughts, though.

The ride back to Kayla's house was mostly quiet. A strange disappointment filled her when she realized that she'd have no reason to talk to Brody anymore. They'd go back to merely being neighbors and ignoring each other whenever possible. She had to admit that she'd enjoyed getting to know him a little better. He'd surprised her with his sensitivity and concern.

But on the other hand, she had so much to be grateful for. This nightmare was finally over.

When they pulled into Kayla's driveway, they both sat in the car for a minute in silence. Finally Madison turned to Brody. "Thank you for everything."

"I'm just glad that you're finally safe again."

She nodded uncertainly before finally putting her hand on the door handle. "Me, too. I guess I'll be seeing you around."

"Let me just walk you inside." He shrugged. "Just to be a gentleman."

They slowly walked side by side to the front door. Even though it was already past six o'clock, Madison knew that Kayla had taken Lincoln to the park. Kayla had been such a godsend during this whole ordeal, and Madison was thankful that her friend had helped pick up the slack some. Now Madison would be able to resume her normal routine again, which meant spending more time with Lincoln.

Madison unlocked the door, unusually aware of Brody behind her. Why did she suddenly feel flustered? The emotion made no sense. When she opened the front door, Brody stepped inside behind her. Madison turned, ready to say good-bye.

The words caught in her throat, however.

Something ticked in the background.

TWELVE

"Stay where you are, Madison." Brody pulled his gun out.

Madison nodded, appearing glued to the spot whether she liked it or not. Her face went pale and her hands gripped the chair molding against the wall.

Brody inched forward, crept toward the sound. *Tick, tick, tick, tick.*

The killer couldn't have come back. He was dead—wasn't he? As Brody skulked down the hallway, the ticking became louder. The sound pulsated in time with his heartbeat.

He paused by the door to the room where Lincoln slept. The ticking appeared to be coming from there. Brody put one hand on the knob and slowly turned, keeping his other hand poised on the gun.

The sound, now louder, clearer, was definitely coming from this room.

Brody's gaze scanned his surroundings. He saw

nothing. Just a messy bed, some strewn clothes and a pile of toys.

His gaze searched for a white egg timer along the surfaces—the dresser, the window sill, the bedpost. Nothing stood out.

He inched along the wall, listening for any telltale sounds of an intruder while trying to find the timer. The ticking was loudest in the corner, amidst a pile of toys and stuffed animals. He kicked a few out of the way. Had the killer buried the egg timer in the middle of this mess?

He didn't see one. One of the toys caught his eyes, though. After one more swipe around the room, he bent down and picked up a dragon. He didn't know whether to chuckle or groan. The ticking had been coming from the toy the whole time.

He kept the dragon in his hand as he went to find Madison. As he rounded to the corner toward the entryway, Brody saw that she was still pressed up against the wall, anticipation seemingly freezing each of her muscles.

He held up the dragon. "Just a toy."

Immediately her body slacked. She shook her head. "Lincoln's dragon. I should have known." She let out an airy laugh and pinched the skin between her eyes. "Wow, am I paranoid or what?"

"Not paranoid. Just cautious. There is a difference."

The two of them stared at each other another

moment. What else was there to say? The case was over and effectively so was their reason to spend any time together. Why did he feel saddened by the thought? And why did he still feel suspicious that the case wasn't truly over?

The conclusion that Alfred was the killer still seemed too easy. Brody was going to keep investigating, even if he had to do it on his own time. He couldn't rest until he was completely sure that Madison and little Lincoln were in no danger.

Madison tucked a strand of hair behind her ear and offered a tight smile. "Well…I guess this is it."

He shuffled his feet, feeling a bit like a schoolboy with a crush at the moment. "I guess it is."

"Thanks for everything you've done. I wouldn't have…" She bit her lip a moment in thought. "I wouldn't have survived without you. Literally."

He stepped forward to leave. Or did he do it to be closer to Madison? At once, the scent of fruity perfume filled his senses. "I'm glad I could help."

Her cheeks turned rosy a moment until finally she moved aside and cleared her throat. "I'll see you around."

He nodded resolutely, breaking from his daze. He cared about Madison. He knew he shouldn't, but he did. "Right. I'll see you." He gave her one last glance before putting his hand on the doorknob. He made sure he twisted the lock in place before he shut the door behind him.

Why did he feel like he was walking away from a piece of his heart?

Madison leaned against the door after Brody left. Her pulse raced out of control. Was it because she'd seen something in Brody's eyes that made her wonder if he was developing feelings for her? Or was it because for the first time since the incident, she was alone? Her heartbeat filled her ears and her throat went dry even thinking about moving from the door.

Madison found it hard to believe that this was truly over and that she was able to return to real life again. Why was her guard still up, then? If Alfred was the bad guy, why did she still feel frightened? She supposed it would take some time to get over everything that had happened to her. She needed to accept that instead of continually fighting it.

She needed to stay at Kayla's tonight, she decided. She wasn't quite ready to return to her house again, though she knew that Lincoln was. She'd work up to it and hopefully, in a couple more days, she'd be ready to face the place where her nightmare had occurred.

Alfred—how could Alfred have been behind all of this? Sure, he had a criminal record and he'd always been a little strange and kept to himself. But a killer? It just didn't make sense to Madison.

She closed her eyes and let her head fall back against the door.

Faith, not fear. That was the lesson she'd heard whispered to her lately. She couldn't make decisions based on her own fears and worries. Instead, she had to live by faith that God was going to take care of her. Though this situation seemed impossible, she had to trust that God was still in control and that He still had a plan. Why was it so much easier said than done sometimes?

Lord, I can't get rid of this fear on my own. Help me to trust You.

Thankfully at that moment she heard a car door slam outside and the sound of little Lincoln giggling as he raced to the door. She smiled. Was he finally safe again? She prayed he was.

The next morning Brody found himself thinking about Madison again and wondering what she was doing. Brody was sure she was probably excited to get back into work and put this whole experience behind her. She'd probably never want to see him again and be reminded of everything that had happened, for that matter. He couldn't blame her.

Brody decided to go back to Alfred's house

again. He wanted to survey the scene himself. Something just didn't feel right to him. It was like all the clues were laid out too perfectly. Someone who'd been that careful when planning his crimes wouldn't leave all the evidence of his guilt out in plain sight. But all Brody had to go on was a gut feeling. Was there any evidence they'd missed that might back up his claim?

Alfred's house was a small brick ranch that was overrun with bushes and trees around the perimeter. One could barely see the place through the foliage. The inside was equally as cluttered.

Brody stood in the middle of the living room and let his gaze circle it. This was the place where they'd found the noose, the pictures, razors, the rough draft of the letters. They were such simple items, items that could have been hidden in a trunk or a dresser drawer. Why would he leave them out the way he did? Something just didn't fit.

Brody flipped through various items in the house. Old magazines, bottles with miniature boats inside, discarded fast-food wrappers. He found nothing to give him insight into the case.

A light knock sounded at the door. Brody glanced over and saw a middle-age woman there, a worried expression showing in the lines around her eyes. Brody motioned her to come in.

"I'm Alfred's neighbor," she introduced herself. "I've heard about everything happening in town, about the murders. I also heard that people are saying Alfred was behind them. Rumors are that the killer made it look like suicide. I heard he used a noose on one of his victims."

"I can't confirm anything right now, ma'am."

"I've been his neighbor for twenty years." She rubbed her hands together, as if nervous. "I keep thinking about the allegations against Alfred, and I felt like I needed to say something."

"Okay."

"You see those boats in the bottles over there?"

Brody nodded, wondering what she was getting at. "Yes."

"Alfred did those himself. It used to be his hobby. But over the past five years his arthritis got bad—really bad. He could hardly even handle giving people change at the register at his store."

"What are you getting at?" he asked curiously.

"If the rumors are true, Detective, and one of the victims had a noose around her neck, Alfred couldn't have done it. He couldn't have tied those knots, not with his hands being in the condition they were."

Brody had a feeling he'd just found the proof he needed that Alfred wasn't their man.

But now he needed to find Madison. She was still in danger.

* * *

Madison knocked on the weathered door of the old boathouse. "Hello?"

No answer. She looked at the paper again. This was the right address. She was supposed to meet a fisherman named Jonas Johnson and take a photo for an exhibit at a local museum. This was a great opportunity for her career, and in the previous weeks before this upheaval in her life, she'd enjoyed capturing photos of locals with their weathered faces and eyes that had seen far more than Madison had in her nearly thirty years. Although it still felt surreal that the danger of the Suicide Bandit was behind her, she'd decided to face life again. She had to get on with her assignments. This was one photo shoot that she was supposed to have turned in yesterday. She'd called Mr. Johnson last night and arranged to come out today, however. She thanked God for people's grace. No doubt he had heard about what had happened to her, as had everyone else in town.

The sun beat down on her and caused a sharp glare off of the waters of the bay. Madison glanced once again at the boathouse. This one was larger than most, situated at the end of a long pier. On one side of the weathered pier was a room where Madison assumed they kept supplies for boating. On the other side appeared, according to the sign on the door, to be a game room. The space was probably the equivalent of a man cave for these fishermen, a place where they could get away from their wives and have a moment to cut loose with their peers.

Madison knocked again. "Mr. Johnson? It's Madison. Are you there?"

She twisted the door handle and it opened. She peered inside. The dark room had drawn shades and smelled musty, like no one had been in there for a while. Maybe it was too hot outside to even use the game room right now.

"I'm back here!" a man yelled.

Madison's eyes darted through the room. Two other doors were inside the room, perhaps to a bathroom or a kitchenette.

Madison sucked in a breath before stepping inside farther. Her attacker was dead, she reminded herself. The nightmare was over. Now she needed to start living without paranoia.

"Come on back!"

She stepped toward one of the doors in the distance. She gripped her camera, trying to calm her racing heart as she dismissed the sudden sweat across her brow, chiding herself for acting irrationally.

As soon as she stepped away from the door, it slammed shut behind her. Total darkness encased her and panic began quivering in her gut before growing into an all-out flail through her entire body. She sucked in a breath and scrambled backward, desperate to find the door frame through darkness so thick it seemed material.

"What are you doing, Madison? You just got here. Why are you in such a hurry to leave?"

The voice caused imaginary bugs to scurry all over Madison's skin.

Her attacker.

He wasn't dead. He was alive, and he was in the room with her.

She tried to back away from the voice, but at once she couldn't figure out where it had come from. Suddenly she lost her sense of direction, couldn't figure out which was way was out or in.

"You're dead. You're supposed to be dead."

"You weren't really naive enough to believe that, were you? Our little game is just beginning, Madison."

"Why? Why me? Why can't you just leave me alone?"

"Because you're my connection to Brody."

"Brody? What's he have to do with this? Besides, he's just my neighbor. That's my only connection."

"But you look just like Lindsey."

"Who's Lindsey?"

"Ask him."

Ask him? Did that mean she'd get out of here alive? "I will. I'll ask him."

The man chuckled. "You really have no clue, do you?"

"I guess I don't. Why not just go directly to Brody? Why go through me?"

"To hurt him." The man's voice seemed to come from the other side of the room. Madison twirled, trying to locate the monster before he lunged.

"Hurting me doesn't hurt him."

"That's what you think. Brody's got to learn a lesson. He's got to learn to stop hurting people."

Keep him talking, Madison thought urgently. "How has he hurt people?"

"He's hurt people badly. Thinks only of himself, not of how his actions will affect others." Again the man's voice moved behind her. Madison felt like the whole room was spinning. She pinched between her eyes, trying to get a grip on reality, to stay in control.

Madison had a hard time thinking of Brody fitting that description. But now wasn't the time to argue with this man.

"What do you want me to do? I really don't understand." She backed up, trying to feel for something to use as a weapon, something to help her protect herself.

Instead a hand wrapped around her mouth from

behind. She tried to scream but couldn't. She tried to thrash, but the man's other arm circled around her midsection, pinning her arms. "What I want you to do is to send him a message. I want you to tell him that revenge is the sweetest weapon, and that this isn't even close to being over."

Then the man jammed something into her neck. A needle. And Madison's world went black.

THIRTEEN

Madison forced her eyes open. Blinked. Tried to focus.

Where was she? What had happened?

Everything flooded back. She gulped in a breath.

Everything was black, so much so that she couldn't make anything out. Was she still in the boathouse? Was her attacker still here?

She closed her eyes and tried to make a mental assessment of herself. Nothing hurt. Her hands were free. Her mouth was uncovered. Nothing circled her neck. Everything around her was quiet. She remained still, waiting to hear the tell-tale sign that someone else was in the room.

Nothing. Not yet. But her attacker was calculating. He could be waiting for her to stir, waiting to take her by surprise again.

She waited longer but heard nothing.

Finally she moved. It took her a moment to find her footing. Whatever the man had injected her with made her wobbly, woozy. She leaned against the wall to steady herself. She'd feel her way around the perimeter of the room until she found the door, she decided.

Her breathing felt labored, almost as if the room itself tried to suffocate her. The darkness felt blinding. She had to get out of here. She had to find Brody and tell him what happened, tell him the madman was still on the loose.

Her hand hit something and it crashed to the floor, shattering. A picture maybe? She stepped over it and continued feeling her way around the room. Finally her hand connected with something metallic. The doorknob. She grabbed it and twisted, but it didn't move.

Using both hands, she shook the door. Why wouldn't it open?

She kicked the wood, tears popping into her eyes as she did so. It was no use. She was locked in here.

She leaned her forehead against the door. How would she get out?

The heat felt stifling, hanging heavy in the air.

A window? Could she open a window? If she could propel herself through it, she would land in the bay below and could swim to shore.

She felt her way around the room again. At last she felt the heavy drapes that covered the windows. Her fingers fumbled as she shoved them aside.

Why didn't light flood the room when she moved the shades? She knew the answer before her hands felt the board that covered the window. She pounded at the wood, hoping it might budge. Nothing.

Was she trapped inside this room? Was there any other means of escape?

She wouldn't give in to despair.

But she wanted to. She wanted to curl into a ball and cry.

No, she needed to keep searching for a means to escape.

Her cell phone! She could call someone.

She reached for her pocket, but it was empty. He had taken her phone. Of course he had. He'd thought of everything else, hadn't he?

There had been two other doors in the room. Where did they lead? She continued around the room. Finally she felt another doorknob. She twisted, but nothing moved. It was locked, also. Of course. A few feet over she found the other door, but as she expected she couldn't open that door, either.

Perhaps she could find something to knock down the outside door? She wasn't strong, but at least she could try. Maybe there was something she could wedge between the door and the frame that would help her. She couldn't give up hope. Who would ever find her here, after all? Was her assignment at this location ever real? Or had the killer simply strung her along? She had a feeling the latter was true. Had she even told Kayla where she was going? No. Only that she was going to take pictures for a new exhibit at the museum. No one was going to find her in this secluded location.

She needed to think. She slid down the wall and pulled her knees to her chest. Just a moment to think. But every moment of entrapment teetered on the edge of turning into despair.

Brody raced down the road toward Madison's house. He gripped the cell phone in his hand and waited for Kayla to pick up the phone at the preschool. Finally on the third ring, she answered. "Kayla, have you heard from Madison?" he asked.

"Madison? No, I haven't talked to her since this morning."

"She's not answering her cell phone and she's not at her house. This isn't like her."

"That is weird. We always ask parents to keep their cell phones with them while their kids are at school in case we need to get in contact with them. You're right—it isn't like her to not answer."

Brody's gut had been churning all day, a sure sign that something was wrong. They'd all been duped into thinking that York County was safe again. In truth the killer remained at large. Brody felt certain of it.

"Kayla, can you keep an eye on Lincoln for a while?"

"Of course."

"I'm going to go and see if I can find Madison. I have a bad feeling."

Kayla looked pale as she nodded. "I pray she's okay, Brody."

He managed a stiff nod. "Me, too."

He went to his car and started toward her house. Each inch closer he got, the more worry embedded itself in his muscles. Madison would never be irresponsible when it came to Lincoln. Never. He knew her well enough already to know that.

As soon as he turned onto their street, he saw that her car wasn't at the house. He had a key to her place. She'd given him her spare just a couple of days ago. He needed to go inside and see if he could figure out where she'd gone.

All was quiet inside her home. He remembered the last time he'd entered unannounced. He'd stumbled upon the horrific sight of Madison hanging from the fan. Tension gripped him at the thought.

"Madison?"

No answer.

He checked all of the rooms and found no one, which was both a relief and a concern.

He went into her office and walked over to her desk. An appointment book lay open in front of the computer. He saw a noon appointment with a Mr. Johnson. Who was Mr. Johnson? She'd mentioned being commissioned to take photos of fishermen in the area for a museum exhibit. Could Mr. Johnson be a part of that? And where would that fisherman live?

He flipped through the rest of her appointment book, searching for an address. Nothing.

He wiggled the mouse on her computer and the screen came up. Directions from a website stared at him. Good old Madison. She hated GPS and always did things old school. That just might work to her advantage right now.

He printed a copy of those directions and ran out to his car. He turned the emergency lights on as he sped down the road. He had a feeling he didn't have any time to waste. And if he did, then he'd rather find out sooner than later that she was okay.

Lord, if You're out there, watch over Madison.

He would never forgive himself if something happened to her.

He sped down the road, praying again that he was on time.

* * *

Madison fought panic. How long had she been here? It felt like hours. Perhaps it had only been minutes? It was hard to say.

Her eyes had adjusted slightly to the darkness, enough that she could make out the outline of a pool table, a couple of chairs, two windows.

She'd run out of ideas as to how else she could get out of here. She wasn't strong enough to bust through the door. There appeared to be no other means of escape. The wood nailed across the windows was stuck and wouldn't even budge.

Despair threatened to overtake her. She tried to steady her breathing.

Lord, help me. I don't know what else to ask except for Your intervention right now. Help someone to realize where I am.

A noise outside brought her to her feet. What was that? Tires on gravel? It was hard to tell over the lapping of the water underneath the pier. Seizing the opportunity, began pounding on the door.

"Help! Someone help me! Please!"

She stopped, listened for a moment. Nothing. Had she been hearing things? What if it was the serial killer, coming back to finish what he'd started?

She decided to risk that possibility and began pounding on the door again, yelling for help and praying that someone would hear her.

She paused again, desperate to hear a sign of life. "Madison? Are you in there?"

Brody! Brody had found her. Hope filled her heart.

"I'm here. I'm in here, Brody!"

The doorknob rattled.

"He's got you bolted in from the outside. A padlock. I'm going to have to knock the door down. Back up for me."

"Got it."

She stepped well out of the way. A moment later she heard a crash against the door. Wood splintered. Then she heard another crash. This time more panels cracked and a ray of sunlight filled the room. Brody shoved the rest of the door out of the way and stepped inside. At once, his arms engulfed her. She savored the feeling of safety, of strength.

His lips found hers in a surprising kiss. She froze a moment before surrendering to the emotions pulling them together. All her worries melted away as the feeling of being cared for radiated through her. All too soon, Brody drew back and rested his forehead against hers.

"I was so worried," he mumbled.

Madison's heart still raced—from both the kiss and the life-or-death situation she'd just encountered. "I didn't know if anyone would find me."

"Of course I'd find you. I'll always find you."

He pulled away and studied her closely. "Are you okay? Did he hurt you?"

She touched her neck where the man had injected her with something. "He drugged me again. I don't think he meant to hurt me. He's just playing this twisted game and, for some reason, I'm a pawn."

His arms wrapped around her again, holding her tight. She rested her head under Brody's chin, surprised at how natural it felt. Then she felt Brody stiffen.

"What is it?" She stepped back and saw him looking at something beyond her. She turned and saw words had been scratched into the wall, almost as if with a knife. She drew in a sharp breath as she read the words.

Death. Selfish. Suicide. Accusation. Hatred Blood.

Brody's hand circled her arm. "Come on. Let's get you out of here. I'm going to call in some backup."

Madison needed to ask him about that kiss sometime, ask him what it meant. But not now. Right now they needed to concentrate on finding this madman. Maybe he'd left some evidence this time. She doubted it, but there was always a chance.

"We need to have you looked at also."

She shrugged. "I'm fine."

"You don't know what he injected you with. You should be checked out."

"I need to get to Lincoln."

"Kayla has him." He led her away from the pier and toward his car. "Let's get some AC on you. I have a bottle of water in here. You need to drink some."

She didn't argue. She let the cool air chill her skin, relishing the current blowing from the vent. Brody handed her some water and she gulped it down, thirstier than she thought. Brody stayed outside the car, on his phone. She could only imagine the conversation he was having.

Her lips still tingled from their kiss. What had that been about? It had been so surprising. Even more surprising was her reaction. What had she been thinking? The last thing she wanted in her life was romance. But based on the way she'd responded to Brody, no one would ever guess that to be true.

Just then Brody opened the car door and slid inside. "Backup is coming, as is the forensic team." His eyes softened as he looked across the seat at her. "Are you sure I can't take you to the hospital?"

She nodded. "I just want to go home. See Lincoln."

"I understand."

The madman's words flooded back to her. "He mentioned you, Brody."

His eyebrows twitched. "Me?"

"He told me to ask you about Lindsey."

Brody's face drained of color. "Lindsey?"

"Who's Lindsey, Brody?"

"She's…she's someone I dated a few times up in New York."

"What's her connection to this case?" she prodded.

"I'm not sure. Except that she committed suicide. I have no idea how this man knows about her death or why he's connecting it with these murders."

"There's obviously something about you and about her that ties all of these things together that have been happening lately. Did you make some enemies after her suicide?"

He sighed deeply. "I was my biggest enemy after her suicide."

"What do you mean?"

"I mean, I blamed myself. I still blame myself. Her suicide note made it clear that she took her life because she couldn't deal with the pain from my rejection."

Madison placed her hand on his arm, but he pulled away. "You can't blame yourself for someone else's actions."

"I didn't want to commit or be tied down. I

think six months was my longest relationship. I didn't consider people's feelings the way I should have. I only thought about myself."

Another sheriff's car pulled up, effectively cutting their conversation off. Maybe it was better that way. Madison had a lot to process. But before she could begin to process any of it, she had to recount what had happened to her.

Brody squeezed her hand. "You ready for this?"

She nodded. "We've got to catch this guy before he strikes again."

"I know." He nodded toward Sheriff Carl outside. "Let's go see what kind of evidence he left."

FOURTEEN

After the entire boathouse had been canvassed for evidence, Brody climbed back into the car with Madison. She looked exhausted. She'd been through a lot, not only today but over the past several days. He needed to get her home to rest.

"Anything?"

Brody shrugged, not wanting to tell her the blunt truth that there appeared to be no evidence of who this man was—no fingerprints, no hairs, no fibers. "We collected a few things we're sending to the lab."

"They won't turn up anything."

"You never know," he reminded her.

"Well, I'm going with my gut. And it's telling me not to get my hopes up."

With a terse nod, he started down the road. "Back to Kayla's, right?"

"I promised Lincoln we could go home tonight. I thought Alfred was the one…"

"I don't know if staying at your house is a good idea, Madison."

"I'm not safe anywhere, Brody. He got into Kayla's house while everyone was there. He knows my email address, he knows my cell-phone number, he knows what my photography appointments are." She released a frustrated breath. "Putting my life on hold has done no good. I've gotta do what's best for my son now. He misses being home."

"I can't let the two of you stay there alone. Especially since I know I'm the reason why this man is coming after you. I'll never forgive myself if something happens to you or Lincoln."

Madison rested a hand on his arm. "We're not responsible for other people's actions, Brody. The only person guilty here is the one doing the crimes."

Brody's lips pulled into a tight line. Madison knew he wasn't buying it. She wouldn't be able to convince him otherwise. That was something between himself and God.

"Let me stay at your place tonight."

"I don't know what kind of example that would be to Lincoln."

"I'll stay on the couch. Kayla can stay over, too, if that would make you more comfortable," he said. "I just know that I don't want the two of you there alone. A deputy sitting in the driveway isn't enough. I want someone nearby at all times."

Madison heard the genuine worry in his voice, and knew that if she tried to get him to stay away it would kill him. "Okay. I'd probably feel better if you were there, too."

They pulled up to a stoplight and Madison's gaze traveled out the window. What a nightmare. She pushed aside the temptation to ask "Why me?" Instead, she blurted, "Poor Lincoln. He deserves so much more than this."

"Hey." Brody gently lifted her chin. "Lincoln is one lucky boy to have you as a mom."

"That's sweet of you to say."

"I'm not trying to be sweet. I'm being honest."

Madison's cheeks flushed. "I just feel like everything is a mess. I feel like everything that's happened is making him grow up too fast. I don't want him to lose that innocence of youth. But I'm not sure how to stop that from happening. Everything feels like it's out of my hands…"

"The Madison I know would say that everything is out of her hands. But it's in God's hands."

She smiled, the truth of his words soaking in. "You're right. That's exactly what I need to keep believing. Thanks for the reminder."

He released his hand from her chin. Madison realized how quickly her heart was beating. Why did Brody have this effect on her? And what exactly was happening between them? Why did her heart want to flip with joy while her brain warned her to put on brakes? He was not the kind to commit or settle down. Getting too close to him would only be setting herself up for heartbreak.

So why couldn't she keep her distance?

Madison stared down the hallway at the door leading to her bedroom. She didn't want to go in there. But she would have to eventually. There was no putting it off.

While Brody checked the rest of the house, her hand went to the knob. She lifted up a prayer before twisting it. When she opened the door, she expected to see the ceiling fan still on the floor, surrounded by broken pieces of ceiling and a dusting of plaster everywhere.

Instead she found clean carpet, a new fan, glossy surfaces. "What...?"

"I hope you don't mind. I probably should have asked first. I knew it would be hard for you to see the room, so I took it upon myself to clean it up and get you a new fan."

"Wow. When did you do all of this?"

"Last night. I couldn't sleep, anyway." He raised an eyebrow. "Did I overstep my bounds?'

"No. I mean, this was incredibly thoughtful. Thank you."

He pressed something into her hand. "Here's the new key to the house. I had all of the locks changed. Someone's coming later this week to install a security system."

"Brody, I can't afford a security system. That's kind of you, but—"

"I'm paying for it."

She shook her head. "I can't let you keep doing that."

"Why not?"

"Because this is my responsibility," she said.

"Why can't I help you? I'm the link here. I'm part of the reason why you're in this situation. You can at least let me help keep you safe." He grasped the sides of her arms and lowered his voice. "Look, I don't expect anything from you. I don't expect you to pay me back. I don't even expect you to be nice to me. I just want to be able to sleep at night. In order to do that, I need to know you're safe. So really I'm doing this for myself."

"Well, when you put it that way…" She looked up into his smoldering eyes and finally cracked a smile. "Knock yourself out, then."

He smiled back. "I knew you'd see things my way."

She could see in his gaze that he wanted to lean down and kiss her again. She wanted him to do just that. But instead of letting anything happen, she stepped away. "I need to call Kayla and tell her to bring Lincoln over. It's close to dinnertime."

"I can do that. Why don't you get cleaned up before Lincoln gets here?"

Madison nodded. A shower sounded perfect right now. She needed to get this grime off her. And she needed to get away from Brody who was sending her emotions into a tailspin.

She closed the door to the bedroom and locked it, wishing it was that easy to separate herself from her feelings.

Brody saw Madison stirring a pot at the stove. He didn't know what was going on with him, but he just couldn't seem to get Madison out of his mind. He wanted to do more than protect her. He wanted to be a part of her life.

But he didn't deserve someone like Madison. He didn't deserve anyone period. The draw he had toward her was stronger, at the moment, than his guilt, however.

He approached her at the stove and let his hand rest at her waist as he leaned toward whatever she was cooking. He inhaled the scent of tomatoes, garlic and basil. Comfort food.

"What are you making?"

She glanced back at him and smiled. "Spaghetti with my mother's special sauce."

"Smells wonderful."

She nodded. "Wait until you taste it."

Lincoln and Kayla worked on a craft project in the other room. Kayla had always been so good with kids, so it was a natural fit that she worked at the preschool. He wondered if maybe she'd finally found someone she was interested in with Daniel. The man seemed nice enough and his outgoing nature would balance her quiet, gentle spirit.

The wind blew and sent a rush of leaves and rain onto the roof. Brody thought he'd heard on the news that they could have thunderstorms tonight. Apparently the bad weather had begun to sweep in. He was glad he'd be staying here tonight, safely tucked away on the couch. Not that he would get much sleep. He'd probably be too busy listening for any telltale signs of an intruder. No man was a ghost. Somewhere, somehow he would leave evidence. When he did, Brody would catch him.

Looking back at Madison again, he suddenly had a vision of what it would be like to be married to her. To come home to warm meals, hugs and kisses. To have someone else whose burdens he could carry; to have someone to help carry his burdens, also. To have a reason to want to get out of bed each morning.

He pushed the images away. He was getting

ahead of himself. He was the one who couldn't even handle a relationship that lasted more than six months. He would never want to put Madison in that position, especially not because of Lincoln. He couldn't take chances with her emotions.

Yet she seemed so different from the other women he'd dated in the past. Not only was she beautiful, but she was down-to-earth with a smile that lit up a room and with a heart that filled the whole county. There was nothing not to love about her.

She stepped away from the stove for a moment and handed him some lettuce. "You don't think you're staying here for free, do you?" She grinned, a sparkle in her eyes. "I think that even a certified bachelor can handle making a salad."

Certified bachelor? He'd show her that he could be more than that. He began to chop the lettuce, slowly and carefully. Madison had wandered away from the stove and walked to the dining room where she stood at the window, watching the storm for a moment. The wind had picked up outside and a steady spray of rain hit the side of the house.

"It's really coming down out there, isn't it?" he called from the kitchen.

"We need the rain."

Lightning flashed and the lights at the house flickered. Madison gasped. Brody abandoned the salad and rushed to the dining room. "What is it?"

She backed away from the window, pointing outside. "Out there. On the pier. There was a man."

"A man? Standing on the pier?"

"I only saw him because of the lightning. He was staring right at the house."

He started toward the door. Adrenaline surged through him. He wasn't going to let this guy get away. Not this time. "Lock up behind me and don't let anyone in. Understand?"

She nodded. "Be careful, Brody."

He didn't care about being careful right now. All he cared about was catching this guy.

He grabbed the gun from his holster and stepped into the rain. It was time to capture this creep once and for all.

The rain, almost icy cold despite the heat, hit Brody in the face as soon as he opened the front door. He waited until he heard Madison lock the door behind him before sprinting toward the bay. The man had been standing on the pier across from Madison's house. Was he the killer? Had he come back to taunt Madison some more, only to be discovered because of the lightning?

The wind slapped him in the face, its force so strong that Brody had to fight against it. Water washed into his eyes as he lumbered forward.

Thunder shook everything around him, echoing off of the bay and vibrating through the ground. Where had the man gone?

Brody wiped his eyes, trying to gather his surroundings. As lightning flashed, he saw the outline of a man retreating from the pier and down the road. Brody took off in a sprint. He had to approach the man. He had to put an end to this horrific nightmare that Madison had been living over the past few days—a nightmare that somehow he was responsible for.

Mud sloshed up his leg and suctioned his sneakers to the ground. Thunder pounded from the sky again, this time even louder than before. The storm was upon them and its fury lashed at everything around. It was as if the Creator himself was reaching down from heaven to send a message.

Lightning crackled. It hit close and seemed to electrify the air.

Where had the man gone? He'd been on the street, but Brody hadn't seen him that time. Was he hiding? Had Brody passed him?

Rain soaked through his clothes now, filled every pore and made his hair into whips that slapped his forehead with every step. He stopped a moment, rested with his hands atop his knees. He needed to take note of his surroundings.

Thunder pounded the air again and raised the

hair on his arms. The rain was so thick that its downpour seemed like curtains around him.

He reached the paved portion of the road. Steam rose from the asphalt that had been scorched by the sun earlier in the day.

Lightning zinged through the sky.

There. He spotted the man fleeing, only feet away. Brody could catch him. Then maybe they'd finally have some answers.

FIFTEEN

Madison stood at the dining-room window watching for Brody. Her fingers gripped the curtain, balling the fabric with her fists.

"What's going on?" Kayla approached, still holding scissors and construction paper from her project. A knot twisted the skin between her eyes.

Lincoln thumped into the room also, looking up at Madison with big, round eyes. "Why did Mr. Brody go running out in the rain? I thought you said I couldn't play outside during thunderstorms, that it was dangerous."

Madison knelt in front of her son. "You can't play outside during thunderstorms. It is dangerous. But Mr. Brody had to go do something that was really important. Besides, he's a grown-up. He can make different decisions than little kids can."

"I'm not little. I'm big."

Madison ruffled her son's hair. "You are getting big, but you still can't go outside when it's thundering and lightning." Madison stood and exchanged a worried glance with Kayla.

Was Brody okay? What if the killer had gotten to him? She rubbed her arms, trying to control her racing thoughts. How had she come to care about Brody in such a short amount of time? It didn't make sense.

"Lincoln, do me a favor and pick up all of these coloring sheets. I need Ms. Kayla's help in the kitchen for a moment."

"Okay." Lincoln frowned, letting it be known that he didn't want to help clean up.

Madison and Kayla slipped into the kitchen. Madison lowered her voice. "There was someone outside the house. We wouldn't have seen him except for the lightning."

"Do you think it's your attacker?"

Madison shrugged. "I have no idea. Who else would be staring at the house in the middle of a storm?"

Thunder shook the house. Lightning flashed again. Madison's gaze was drawn to the window. Would she be able to spot Brody?

Lord, watch over him. Please.

Why wasn't he back yet? Was he hurt? Should Madison call the sheriff?

"How about if I call Daniel? He could come out and help? He doesn't live that far away."

"Maybe that's a good idea." Madison couldn't risk going outside herself, not when she considered

Lincoln. She couldn't very well send Kayla out to check on him, either. Perhaps Daniel could help.

Brody should be back by now. He'd had plenty of time to check out the man outside. If the man had been a harmless bystander who just happened to be outside her house, then the confusion would be cleared up by now and Brody would back. But if the man was the town's serial killer...

Madison shivered. She couldn't think about it. Brody was fine.

She walked to the window, waiting for lightning to illuminate her front yard again. Thunder crashed. The lights flickered again.

Madison's throat went dry.

"Mommy?"

She looked down and saw Lincoln, his eyes still wide. She picked him up. "Yes, honey?"

"I'm scared. I don't like thunderstorms."

"Mommy's got you, sweetie. There's nothing to be afraid of." But was her statement even true? She sighed, unable to come up with anything else to say. Instead, she gathered Lincoln close and stared out the window.

Perhaps she should call the sheriff's office to send someone out. But she knew that by the time they arrived here, their help wouldn't make a difference. If Brody needed help, then he needed it now. Kayla had said that Daniel didn't live far away. Hopefully he'd get here soon.

The lights flickered again until the entire house went black. Lincoln whimpered.

"Let me find a flashlight," she told him, wishing she'd thought ahead to have one nearby. The room was pitch black, and the darkness felt blinding enough to take her breath away.

"Do you have any matches? I could light some candles," Kayla said.

"They're in a drawer in the kitchen. You'll have to feel your way there."

Thunder again bellowed. As its fury faded to a rumble, another sound echoed through the house. The door. Someone was knocking at the door. The question was, who?

"Madison, it's me, Brody!"

She pivoted Lincoln on her hip and tried to peer through the peephole. It was no use. Blackness stared back. Of course the voice had belonged to Brody. She flipped the locks and, despite her logic, slowly edged the door open. Relief filled her when she spotted Brody on the other side. He held another man by the arm, though.

"Mr. Steinbeck?"

The two men stepped inside, dripping water all over the entryway. Madison didn't care.

"I got stuck out in the storm," Mr. Steinbeck explained.

"So why were you standing outside staring at the house, then?"

"I was contemplating knocking at your door to see if I could come inside until the storm passed. I thought you might think I was crazy if I did that, though. I parked my car off Seaford Road, so I decided to try and make it back. But my knee gave out in my dash down the road."

Kayla appeared on the scene. "I found the matches. Let me light some candles so we can see. Is everything okay?"

Brody finally released his grasp on Mr. Steinbeck. "Yeah, I think so."

"I heard there's a serial killer in town. I should have used more discretion." Mr. Steinbeck shrugged, looking smaller than usual with his clothes clinging to his narrow frame.

Even Mr. Steinbeck could have a sinister side hiding beneath that kind yet eccentric exterior. Having him in her home made her feel uneasy, even if he did have a decent excuse for his actions. But Brody was here, Madison reminded herself. He would protect them.

Madison took a step toward the bathroom. "Let me get you guys some towels."

Kayla grabbed a candle. "I can do that."

Madison tried to catch Brody's gaze, but darkness still shadowed everything. She wanted to know if he'd been hurt, to know if he bought the story Mr. Steinbeck had told them. He didn't go far away from the fisherman, Madison noticed.

The silhouette of a broad figure appeared in the doorway. Madison nearly leapt out of her skin.

"Everything okay?"

Kayla stepped forward with some towels. "Daniel. Thanks for coming."

Madison glanced at Brody. "We knew we couldn't leave the house, so we called Daniel to come, just in case you were in trouble."

Brody nodded tightly. "We're all fine."

Mr. Steinbeck's eyes widened. "Madison, you were the victim who survived, weren't you?"

Madison heaved in a breath, fighting the urge to freeze up in the face of uncomfortable questions. Why did she keep denying it? What good would that do her?

"Yes, Mr. Steinbeck. I was the victim who survived."

"I was afraid it might have been you. I'm so sorry to hear that. You've always been so kind. You don't deserve to face something like that."

His sincerity warmed her. "Thank you, Mr. Steinbeck."

"I saw a man snooping outside of your house last week."

Madison's pulse quickened. "What do you mean?"

"I'd just returned from fishing and I noticed a man crouching around the outside of your home. I started to go over and question him but he ran off into the woods. My old legs weren't quick enough to keep up with him."

"Do you remember what he looked like? Anything would help," Brody said.

Mr. Steinbeck shrugged. "He seemed young, athletic. The way he darted away from the house made it obvious he was in shape. He seemed tall. Close to six feet probably. He had a hat on and black clothing that covered nearly every inch of skin."

Brody's steely gaze held fast to Mr. Steinbeck. "Did he say anything?"

"Not a word. He just saw me and ran." Mr. Steinbeck shook his head.

"Did he have anything in his hands? A crowbar? A camera? Anything?" Brody asked.

"My eyes aren't that good. I didn't see anything."

Madison rubbed her hands together, just as desperate for answers. "Was that the first time you'd ever seen anyone around the house?"

"First time I ever noticed and I'm out every day. I wished I'd seen something that day you were attacked, Madison. Maybe I could have done something. Called the cops, at least."

"Why didn't you tell the sheriff that you saw someone outside of Madison's house, Mr. Steinbeck?" Brody asked.

"I figured I'd scared him and he wouldn't come

back. I had no idea he was a killer. I'm sorry, Madison. If I'd known, I would have done more. But I had no idea."

"When was that, Mr. Steinbeck?"

"Sunday."

The day before her attack. The killer was obviously plotting Madison's demise. The mere thought of it made her knees start to buckle. Brody's hand gripped her arm, holding her steady. Thank goodness for Brody. He'd kept her from sinking more than once since this whole ordeal began. She could get used to his strength, if she let herself. But she wouldn't. She couldn't, no matter how much she desired to do just that.

"I'd make you guys some coffee, but the power is out," Madison said as they all stood in the dark entryway with water pooling on the floor.

Brody glanced down. "I noticed. I'd settle for simply getting out of these wet clothes."

"I can stick around for as long as you need me to," Daniel spoke up.

Even in the darkness Brody could see Kayla blushing. His cousin was falling hard for the town's local baseball coach. The man seemed decent enough. Brody nodded toward Mr. Steinbeck. "I think we'll be okay here. Would you mind giving Mr. Steinbeck a ride home? That would be a huge help."

"No problem." Daniel glanced at the drenched fisherman. "You'll have to make a dash through the rain to get to my truck, though."

"I don't know about dashing, but I'll get there. Beats walking down the lane in the rain." Mr. Steinbeck turned to Madison. "I'm sorry that I frightened you."

"Don't worry about it. Just get home and take care of yourself."

There Madison was again, acting selfless and kind and putting others before herself. Was there really anything not to love about the woman? Not that he loved her...but the idea was way too tempting at the moment.

Daniel paused at the door and looked back at Kayla. "I'll call you tomorrow. Sound okay?"

She smiled warmly. "Sounds perfect."

Brody pushed aside an image of him and Madison double-dating with Daniel and Kayla. He wasn't even sure where the idea had come from. It just popped into his mind and he'd inadvertently entertained it in there for a couple of minutes too long.

After Daniel and Mr. Steinbeck left, the three remaining adults all looked at each other as if wondering what to do next. No electricity meant no dinner, no shower and no lights to be able to see anything. His clothes had stopped dripping, but the soggy fabric clung uncomfortably to his skin. Since the power was out, the AC wasn't working and the outdoor heat had floated into the house, thickening the air with humidity. The storm had finally begun moving offshore, and the thunder and lightening weren't nearly as violent as earlier.

"I guess this is good practice for hurricane season, huh?" he asked.

"There's already a storm heading through the Caribbean. One of the projected paths takes it right up the coast of Virginia," Madison said. "And since it's your first year here, in case you haven't noticed yet, we have a tendency to flood here so you better find your waders."

Although she tried to sound lighthearted, Brody knew that her nerves were frayed. The scares and threats just kept coming, and she took each one as it came. But how many blows could one person take?

The lights flashed back on at that moment and immediately they heard the AC blowing through the house. "I'm going to go get cleaned up." He nodded toward the shower.

"I'll finish dinner," Madison offered.

"I want to help! I want to help!" Lincoln said, jumping up and down.

Madison smiled and reached out her hand. "Let's go, then."

Brody walked away, enjoying the feeling of having a temporary family a little too much.

That evening, once Lincoln was asleep, Madison wandered back to the living room to speak privately with Brody. He sat on the couch with his elbows perched atop his knees and a serious expression stretched across his face. He straightened as she approached.

For some reason—and against her will—her heart raced.

He stood. "Madison."

As natural as if they'd known each other for years, Madison stepped into his arms—or did he step toward her? She couldn't be sure. She only knew that his arms circled her and she rested her head against his chest. The hammering of his heart seemed to steady her own.

"I was so worried about you today, Madison."

Was she imagining things or did she hear true concern in his voice? Whether real or imagined, tears popped into her eyes at the mere thought of having someone care about her again. For so long she'd pushed aside the notion that she would ever find someone else to take Reid's place. It wasn't that there hadn't been offers, but she'd simply never met anyone she thought she'd want to open up her heart to again. With Brody, it felt different.

He gently placed a kiss atop her head.

She had to talk to him about this thing between them before her emotions got the best of her. "Brody, what are we doing?"

He pulled back, but his hands still remained on her arms, rubbing them affectionately. "What do you mean?"

Being so close to Brody made her throat go dry, made her want to forget this conversation and simply just enjoy the moment. She couldn't do that, though. She had to protect not only her heart but Lincoln's.

She sucked in a deep breath. "I feel like we keep flirting with a...a relationship, I suppose. Maybe a fling. I'm not sure what's going on. I'm not in the same place in life that I was at one time. Lincoln and I are a package deal and I don't want him to get hurt."

"Madison, I'm not looking for a relationship."

Her heart dipped. Of course he wasn't looking for a relationship.

He shook his head and squeezed his eyes shut a moment. "That came out wrong. I mean, I didn't *think* I was looking for a relationship. Deep down I knew I didn't deserve someone like you. But I've never met a woman like you before. You...I know it sounds cliché, but you make me want to be a better person."

She tamped down her fluttered heart. "You've told me about your past, Brody. Maybe I shouldn't bring this up now, but I need to for my sake and Lincoln's. What about your commitment issues?"

His hands dropped from her arms and he took a step back. "I've been thinking a lot about that, Madison. And honestly, even though I had a reputation as a player, I'm not a player. I just always reached a point in my relationships where I realized I couldn't see myself committing to that person. There was no need to keep pretending or to keep dating if we didn't have a true future."

She could admire that. She really could. But she still had more questions. "And six months from now when you discover the same thing about me?"

He shook his head. "I'm not going to."

"How can you be sure?"

He looked in the distance and sucked in a deep breath before meeting her gaze again. "I guess I can't be one-hundred percent sure. The truth is every relationship requires risk. I want to take that risk and see what we've got, see if it's real. In my heart I think it is."

Madison crossed her arms over her chest. What did she tell him? How did she feel? Of course she was attracted to the man. But attraction wasn't enough.

He stepped toward her again and bent his head. "What are you thinking, Madison?"

"My thoughts are racing a million directions

right now." It was the truth. Her emotions seemed to be swirling around in her head, unable to find a safe place to land.

"Can we sit down and talk?"

She nodded and they sat on the couch facing each other. Brody reached out and took one of her hands. Warmth washed through her at the overture. It was so simple, yet so sweet. She hadn't felt emotions like this since…Reid.

The lights in the room were still out and everything around them quiet. Ordinarily the dark and the quiet would frighten her. But with Brody close to her she felt safe. She knew he wouldn't let anything happen to her, that he would sacrifice himself before he let her get hurt. But that wasn't enough to build a relationship on.

"Talk to me, Madison. I'm not trying to toy with your emotions here. I really want to know how you're feeling. If you want me to back off, I will. Just say the word."

His words brought a measure of comfort. He was leaving the ball in her court, telling her that he'd respect any decision she made. But she wasn't sure what decision to make. "I'm not one to jump into things, Brody. I guess I just need some more time to process…everything. These are extraordinary circumstances we've been thrown into."

"I'd agree." He smiled.

Her thoughts churned a million miles a minute. "I'm not sure exactly how to sort through everything I'm feeling. I guess what I really want is to simply get to know you more."

His mouth curled into a half smile. "I can respect that." He lifted her hand and kissed the top of it. "Can I give you a hug, Madison?"

"I'd love a hug right now."

He pulled her toward him and held her. They didn't say anything. And they didn't need to.

SIXTEEN

Madison slept better that night than she had in a while. It helped to know that Brody was on her couch. Still she slipped out of bed early, just as the sun was rising. She quickly dressed and tiptoed into the kitchen to start a pot of coffee. As she passed the front door, she saw the towels still on the floor to catch any puddles of water from last night. All of the clocks in the house blinked from the power outage. But today the sun brightly peeked over the horizon, seeming to promise hope and a better day. Madison knew she wouldn't have a better day until the killer was behind bars, though.

Needing something to keep her occupied, she mixed a batch of blueberry muffins and stuck them in the oven. As they baked, she grabbed some coffee and sat at the dining-room table.

Lord, I need Your strength to get through another day. I'm running out of steam on my own. I want to live in faith, not fear.

"Morning."

Madison looked back and saw Brody lumber into the room. Poor guy didn't look like he'd gotten any sleep last night. He ran a hand over his face and sat across from her. Her heart stammered at the mere sight of him.

She rose. "Let me get you some coffee."

"That sounds great."

Madison hurried into the kitchen and poured him a mug, pulling the muffins from the oven in the process. The scent of the baked goods wafted up to her and she smiled.

"What a night last night, huh?" Brody asked, taking the coffee from her.

"You're telling me. On a positive note, I think Lincoln really enjoyed learning how to play crazy eights with you last night. He said he's going to teach you how to play cornhole sometime."

"Cornhole, huh? I can't wait to learn."

Before their conversation went any further, Brody's cell phone beeped. He pulled it from his belt and answered. Madison watched as he transformed from a laid-back houseguest into a hard-edged cop. When he hung up, his gaze met hers. "The tox screen is back. We know what kind of drug the man injected you with."

Madison grabbed her hands around the coffee mug and squeezed it, probably harder than necessary. "And?"

"It was a drug called Lorazepam."

"I've never heard of it."

"It's a sedative, usually given before surgery or to treat seizures. It can be given in smaller doses to treat anxiety or sleeping disorders."

"How would someone get their hands on something like that? It has to be a controlled substance, especially since it was injected. Not everyone has access to things like that."

"You can buy almost any drug in the world online now without a prescription—illegally, of course." He shrugged. "Or a doctor would have access to it. At least we have a place to look now."

She shifted in her seat. "You said it's used to treat sleeping disorders?"

"Yeah, why?"

"Mark, my reporter friend. He's always talking about having insomnia. Do you think…?"

"We'll look into it." He leaned forward and swiped a hair out of her eye. "Don't worry too much right now. I've got someone watching Mark, just in case he is our man."

She nodded, still pensive.

Brody rested his hand atop hers. "You okay with coming with me today, Madison? I don't want to leave you alone, but I've got to keep investigating."

She remembered her photography appointments, her bills, Lincoln. She needed to spend some quality time with her son. This past week she'd been so focused on catching the killer and dealing with other stress that they'd spent little time together. "Lincoln needs me. I feel like an absentee mom lately."

"He knows you love him. I can see it in the way you interact with each other. Soon this case will be behind us and things will return to normal. It seems impossible right now, but this will end." He gazed intently at her. "In order to keep Lincoln safe, I've got to keep you safe."

"I owe Kayla big time. I don't even know if she can watch Lincoln again today. I probably should have just sent him down to stay with my parents, but I just didn't want them to stress out over what was happening. Especially since my dad has a heart condition."

He nudged her chin up. "You're doing the right thing. And Kayla doesn't seem to mind. She mentioned that she had to go to the church today and work on a bulletin board. I'm sure Lincoln could go with her."

Madison sighed, still feeling burdened. "And aside from Lincoln, I don't know if I can afford to miss work. Actually, there's no 'I don't know' about it. I can't afford it." She rubbed her temples, suddenly overwhelmed.

Brody put his hand on her knee. "We can squeeze some of your appointments in between what I need to do. I don't want you going any-where alone, though. Not until this man is caught. It's too apparent that he's got his eyes set on you."

She nodded heavily. "You're right. I'll just bring my laptop and work on some of the images I've taken lately. I can email some digital proofs to my clients."

"No problem. Can you be ready in thirty?"

She nodded and placed the coffee mug in the sink. "I better get busy."

She started to walk away when he tugged at her arm. She paused and looked at him.

"One more thing. There's a crew coming over today to install that security system and cameras around your house. If the Suicide Bandit comes back, I want to see what he looks like, how he moves, what he's doing."

She shivered, but didn't argue. "Okay." She had moments of feeling normal, but just as quickly as they appeared, reality dropped like a hundred-pound brick, crushing her temporary peace.

She closed her eyes, tired of living under this fear.

Faith, she remembered. She was supposed to be a person of faith. But instead of trusting God, she'd let fear invade every second, it seemed.

She'd start working on that faith today. And she'd start by trusting that God would provide for them, even when she wasn't able to complete all of her photography jobs.

Faith, not fear, she repeated to herself as she got ready. Faith, not fear.

While Brody made phone calls and consulted other detectives in the office, Madison worked on her computer, cropping photos and fixing various problems. She needed to send the baseball pictures to Coach Daniel and some of the real-estate photos to the agency who'd hired her.

"Do you work on your photos in public a lot?"

Madison looked up and saw Brody staring at her from his desk. Her heart sped at the sight of him, as it did every time. His perceptive, warm green eyes watched her. The hard lines of his muscles pulled taut against his shirt, showing off his well-sculpted frame. His thick hair looked tousled, as if he'd just run his hand through it. The sight of the wayward strands made Madison want to reach over and comb her fingers through the mess. Why did the man have to have that effect on her? She almost wished that she felt nothing toward the man. Life would be much simpler that way.

She thought about his question a moment before shrugging. "It depends. If I'm out and between assignments I might stop by a coffeehouse to work for a little while. Why?"

"You know it's possible that someone could have jumped on your network and grabbed your pictures from there."

"Really? People can do that? I have a firewall."

"Yeah, but when you jump onto another connection, you open yourself up to all kinds of threats."

"So what you're saying is that Mark may not be the bad guy here? It could have been anybody."

His expression remained grim. "That's exactly what I'm saying." He let out a breath and a glimmer of hope returned to his eyes. "I do have some good news, though."

"What's that?"

"There are some drugs missing from the hospital in Newport News."

Madison straightened. "That's the one where I was treated after my attack."

"It is. There's more to it. The doctor who treated you used to live in Brooklyn."

"Coincidence?"

"Maybe…maybe not," he said. "I'm going to go with Detective Blackston to question him. The man definitely had a connection to the nurse. Apparently Deputy Victor had given him a speeding ticket once, so the man has affiliations with some of the victims. We'll see if any of this pans out."

"Can I tag along?"

He shook his head. "Not a good idea. I think you should stay here."

Madison frowned, though she understood.

"I won't be gone long. You going to be okay here?"

"I'll be fine," she insisted.

The good doctor checked out. For a majority of the times the attacks occurred, the doctor's time was accounted for and verified by several people. Plus, there was no way the doctor would have been able to get from Madison's house after her attack back to the hospital to treat her in time. Just another dead end.

Brody sighed. He wished he had some good news to take back to Madison, but he didn't.

As he drove back to the station, deep in thought, he knew he was falling for the woman. Falling like he hadn't fallen in a very long time.

He thought about the happiness that he saw in her. It seemed to come from a place much deeper than just external pleasures. She was content at her core. He admired that, even desired that for his own life.

Before he went back to the sheriff's office, he called the men he'd hired to install the security system. The man who owned the company had done the job himself and told Brody that they were finished. Brody decided to swing by the station to pick up Madison and then head over to the house to check everything out.

He couldn't help but notice that Madison's face lit up when she saw him. Maybe she did feel the same way about him that he felt about her. He wanted to tread carefully when it came to a relationship with her. He had so much baggage. Had he really let go of it? Or was he simply ignoring his underlying issues because his feelings for Madison superseded everything else at the moment? He didn't know for sure, but it was something to keep in mind.

"It looks like you made out okay while I was gone." He noted the Chinese food on his desk.

"Bonnie stopped by for a visit. She was kind enough to bring lunch. Just left a few minutes ago."

Brody smiled. Sheriff Carl's wife was always kind and gracious. "I need to stop by your house for a few minutes. Want to come?"

"Absolutely."

Madison slipped her hand into his outstretched one. Her soft skin made his heart lurch unexpectedly. He forced himself to let go after he helped her to her feet.

After they were snug in his car, air conditioning blaring, Madison turned to him. "What about the doctor?"

"He's clear."

She sighed and leaned back into the seat. "So we're back to square one?"

"It appears. I even did a background check on your reporter friend Mark."

"And…?"

"Aside from one arrest in college for drunk and disorderly conduct, his record is clear. There's nothing that would indicate he's involved in any of this."

Madison shook her head. "Sometimes I don't feel like this is ever going to end."

"We're getting closer and closer every day. I know it doesn't seem like it, but we are. Just hang on."

As they pulled onto their street, Brody followed Madison's gaze to the pier.

"Mr. Steinbeck's not out there today," she mumbled.

"We probably scared him away."

"I don't think I ever remember him missing a day out there during the summer and any other day when school's not in session. He lives to fish and be on the water. It's only too bad he couldn't afford his own place on the bay."

"It's nice that you let him use yours," he murmured.

"It was practically written in the contract before we bought the house. The previous owners thought the world of him, and begged us to let him continue using it. Reid and I didn't care." She shrugged. "He can be a little rough around the edges, but he's never been a problem. I'm just sorry he got pulled into the mess last night."

"I think he'll recover. In fact, maybe that's exactly what he's doing this morning—resting."

"Maybe I'll make him some soup. I know he lives alone and it's always nice to have someone watching out for you on days when you're under the weather."

The woman seemed to have a heart of gold. She constantly thought of others before she thought of herself. Brody never thought he could be that selfless. But when he thought about Madison and Lincoln, he knew more than anything that he wanted them to be safe and cared for. Something about them made him want to protect them, to support them and provide for them. He would go without sleep, food, shelter, whatever it took if he knew they were safe.

They pulled into Madison's driveway. Brody's gaze searched the surroundings as they walked up to the house. Everything appeared in place. Until this madman was caught, Brody vowed to stay on guard at all times, however.

They stepped inside, and he turned to Madison. "Stay here for a minute."

She nodded, and Brody checked out the rest of the house. Everything appeared clear. He met her in the entryway again and reached for her hand. "Let me show you this new system."

He led her into the dining room where the monitor for the outside cameras had been set up. He sat at one chair and she pulled up a seat beside him.

"It's going to take me a few minutes to figure this system out," he told her.

"I'll start some soup, then."

He read the instructions that the installer had left. In the other room Madison hummed in the kitchen as pots and pans banged around. Something about the scenario felt right, something about the two of them sharing the same space, working side by side, sharing their thoughts and feelings.

Oh, man, he had it bad. He shook his head and kept reading the instructions. Finally Madison came and sat beside him again. He was keenly aware of her presence, so much that the words began blurring across the paper for a moment. He forced himself to focus.

"Let's take a test drive of these cameras."

Madison stared at the screen. "So the cameras are on all the time? Recording everything that goes on outside?"

"That's right. If the Suicide Bandit comes back, we'll see him."

He rewound the video feed. The crew had left

two hours ago after installing the cameras and Brody had asked them to go ahead and start recording. He'd gotten a brief lesson on how the system worked over the phone. Now he wanted to put that knowledge into action.

Madison's backyard showed up on the screen.

"That's my yard with the grass that desperately needs to be cut," Madison said with a smile.

"I can help you with that."

He switched cameras and the front yard showed up, then switched again and saw the side yards, which included a view of his own home. It felt like forever since he'd actually lived in that house, but he didn't mind. There were more important matters at stake.

The feed switched back to the front yard again.

"Seems pretty simple," Madison said. "I can't possibly pay for this, Brody. It looks expensive."

"You're not paying for it, Madison. You didn't ask for the system to be put in, so it's not your responsibility. I'm doing this as a part of the investigation."

And it would cost him a pretty penny, but he wasn't concerned about it. All he cared about was that Madison was safe and in order for her to be safe, they had to catch this guy.

Madison clutched his arm, her gaze widening as she stared at the screen. "What's that?"

He leaned toward the monitor. A man wearing

black slunk against the brick at the back of the house. The time stamp told him the recording had taken place an hour ago.

"It's him," Madison whispered, her grip on his arm tightening. "He was here. Today."

Brody watched the man, who was cloaked in all black from head to toe. Once the man rounded the corner of the house, he paused. Then the man stepped away from the house. His head tilted toward the camera.

The ski mask the man wore only showed his eyes. Despite that, Brody was quite certain that the man was smiling.

Chills raced through him. The Suicide Bandit was more sinister than Brody had imagined. And coming from a New York City detective that said a lot.

SEVENTEEN

Madison poured herself another cup of coffee but the chills wouldn't go away. The image of the man outside her home seemed a permanent stain on her thoughts. She lowered herself onto the couch beside Brody and slowly released the air she held in her lungs.

She shook her head. "He's mocking us, isn't he? He knew we had the cameras installed and he came by just to let us know that he's a step ahead of us."

Brody ran a hand through his hair, leaving strands of it standing on end. "That's certainly how it seems."

"He has no fear. It was broad daylight again when he came by. He must be watching the house, just waiting for appropriate times to terrorize me."

Brody slipped his arm around her and pulled her toward him until her head rested against his chest. She didn't argue. In fact, she welcomed the embrace. She listened for a moment to the steady rhythm of his heart. The beat seemed to calm down her own racing pulse.

In the kitchen the soup boiled and the lid clanged against the pot in protest. The coffee-pot grunted as the last bit of liquid percolated. The oven beeped, telling her it was ready for the brownies she'd whipped up earlier. Everything felt so normal. Yet nothing was normal.

The crime-scene unit was on their way to see if the man had left any evidence. Madison already knew that he hadn't. He never did. Brody had found a couple of footprints around the outside of her house, thanks to the storm last night softening up the ground. But the footprint could have been left from the crew that had been over to install the cameras. It was hard to tell.

At least they had an image of the man from the camera. Certainly that would help the police… wouldn't it? It verified, at least, that the man was built solid, that he was medium-tall, that he was probably fairly young and in good shape. That could describe a lot of people in town, though. Besides, the man didn't even have to be from Seaford. There were surrounding communities where thousands of people lived, thousands of people, any of whom could be to Seaford in twenty minutes or less.

She needed to think about something else—anything else besides the killer.

She squeezed her eyes shut. Tomorrow was Sunday. Church day.

And tomorrow after church was the congregation's annual summer cookout. How could she have forgotten? Lincoln had been looking forward to it, mostly because of the cornhole tournament that would take place there. She groaned and leaned her head against Brody.

"What is it?"

"It's nothing. I just promised Lincoln we could go to the church picnic tomorrow. The last thing I feel like doing is being social right now, not with everything that happened." She hadn't felt like being social much since Reid had died, if she were to be honest with herself.

"It might be good for you, help you to feel halfway normal for a while. Of course with the hurricane coming, the whole event could be cancelled."

"We never cancel our church picnics." She smiled, saying the words lightly even though they were true. "Nothing comes between our congregation and food." She turned toward him. "You should come."

"Me—to church? I can't even remember the last time I set foot inside a church building."

"Then it's time you do."

"People will think I've lost my mind, that I have no place there."

"You're wrong. People will be thrilled to see you. Pastor Ray would love to meet you. I don't know what you've done in the past, but there's nothing that God can't forgive."

He stared at her a moment, and Madison tried to read the emotions that passed through his eyes. Finally, he kissed her forehead and pulled her toward him again. "Thank you, Madison."

Madison wasn't exactly sure what he meant, but her heart soared. Maybe he would finally let go of his past and embrace God.

After the crime-scene unit left, Madison turned to Brody. "I need to go get Lincoln. Kayla's been an angel throughout all of this, and I'm so thankful to her. It helps that Lincoln adores her."

Brody leaned forward with his elbows on his knees. "How about if we drop the soup off at Mr. Steinbeck's on the way there?"

"That would be perfect."

Madison divided the soup into two large containers—one for them and one for Mr. Steinbeck. She hoped he liked chicken noodle. Soup always made her feel better. She placed the containers in two bags and added crackers and brownie squares.

They locked up the house and Brody helped her

to carry the containers to the car. The wind had picked up since they were outside earlier, a sure sign of the coming storm. The forecast said that Hurricane Gabe was headed up the coast at the moment. It would probably diminish some by the time it reached Virginia's coast, but the storm was sure to saturate everything, maybe even down some trees.

Mr. Steinbeck's house wasn't far from Madison's—just down the lane where she lived and three blocks over. It was smallish with only a kitchen, living room and one bedroom. Madison had stopped by once before, right after she'd moved in, to let Mr. Steinbeck know that he could still use her pier.

Brody's cell phone rang as they traveled. Madison waited until he'd hung up to ask about the hardened looked on his face. "Everything okay?"

"That was Daniel."

"What did he want?"

"He read the article your reporter friend Mark wrote for the newspaper. As he was reading, something occurred to him that he thought could help us."

"What was that?"

"He said that all of the crimes took place at a time when school was out. One over Memorial Day weekend, another on a teacher work day and the rest during the summer."

"So he thinks the killer might be an employee of the school system?" she mused.

"It's something worth exploring."

"Mr. Steinbeck..."

Brody glanced over at her and nodded. "I know. He drives a school bus."

As they pulled into the driveway of Mr. Steinbeck's rundown home, Madison shivered. She spotted a car in the driveway. Good, Mr. Steinbeck might still enjoy the soup while it was fresh and warm. But was he guilty? Could he really be the killer?

Brody stepped out of the car with her. He was never far away and Madison had to admit that she appreciated it. Having him close felt good. It felt good to feel protected and cared for, even if she had no business feeling that way about him. She wished she wasn't drawn to the man, but she had to admit that she was, like it or not.

At the moment, she liked it.

She picked up a copy of today's newspaper from Mr. Steinbeck's porch and rapped at the door. Several minutes passed with no answer. Madison glanced at Brody. "What do you think?"

"Maybe he's around back. Can't hurt to check."

Carefully Madison stepped over the broken bricks on his front steps and walked across the cracked sidewalk to the chain-link fence at the side of his house. "Mr. Steinbeck?" she called.

Still no response.

His backyard looked just as neglected as the front. Despite all of the junk, Madison still didn't see the fisherman.

"You could always leave the food on the front porch. I'm sure he'll be back soon. Maybe he just went on a walk or something. The food should be okay for a couple of hours."

As they walked back toward the front door, Madison glanced up at the window at the side of the house. She screamed and dropped the food. The container opened and soup splashed everywhere.

It didn't matter. Mr. Steinbeck wouldn't be eating anything tonight.

He was hanging from the ceiling fan in his living room.

Despite the heat, Brody slipped a blanket around Madison's shoulders. The killer wasn't even bothering to try and disguise the crimes through different suicide methods. He'd killed Mr. Steinbeck the way he'd tried to kill Madison.

She leaned against his sedan and stared at Mr. Steinbeck's house, her skin pale and lifeless. He rubbed her arms a moment before pulling her into a hug.

"Are you okay?"

"I don't know," she answered, her voice listless.

"I'm sorry you had to see that."

"I'm sorry Mr. Steinbeck is dead."

"Everyone called him Fillet," he pointed out. "No one thought of him as 'William.'"

Her gaze met Brody's, life suddenly returning to her eyes. "What did this note say?"

Brody swallowed, his throat dry. "The usual."

"That's not what I mean. What name did it spell?"

"It's not important."

Fire flashed in her eyes. "Of course it is. Brody, what aren't you telling me?"

He pulled back and drew in a deep breath. "You don't want to know, Madison."

"Brody…"

He drew his lips together in a tight line. "Madison, the note spelled my name. It spelled 'Brody.'"

The next morning as Madison sang about "Amazing Grace," all she could think about was the suicide note left at Mr. Steinbeck's house. She felt herself go pale every time she thought about the message left within the note.

Brody.

Her heart squeezed at the thought. Not Brody. *Please, Lord, not Brody.*

Brody stood beside her as they sang. He looked

surprisingly comfortable considering everything he'd told Madison about never being a regular churchgoer. Lincoln stood on the other side of her, occasionally finding the right word to sing but mostly staring at everyone around him. Before they sat down, the boy scooted around Madison and plopped himself between her and Brody. Madison couldn't help but smile, thrilled that her son liked Brody. Nobody could ever replace Reid, but Lincoln certainly needed some male role models in his life. Brody seemed to be that person.

Or could he be a father figure to Lincoln? Madison chewed on her lip at the thought. The idea was gradually becoming one that she could grow to like. God was changing her heart because there was a time when she'd been totally closed to the notion of filling the void in her life. She'd thought she could never love again. But what if she could?

At the end of the song they all took their seats as Pastor Ray started his sermon. Madison's gaze roamed the congregation. It didn't seem to matter where she was—she never felt safe anymore, not even at church. Would she ever feel safe again?

She thought about Kayla and Daniel. The two of them seemed happy and content and settling into couple mode. Seeing them together made Madison's heart flutter with the reminder of what new love was like.

Brody stretched his arm behind Lincoln, glancing down to grin at the boy in the process. Madison didn't miss how Brody's gaze swept over her also. He seemed to approve of the blue-striped sundress she'd picked for this morning. Against her will, pleasure warmed her cheeks.

She didn't want to admit it, but Kayla and Daniel weren't the only couple on the verge of a blossoming relationship. Madison knew that she felt those stirrings with Brody also. She pushed aside the thoughts to concentrate on the sermon. But between her confusion about her feelings and her fear for Brody's life, she barely heard a word the pastor said.

"You've got to try some of Mildred's fried catfish. It's a classic at church picnics. Best in Seaford. Hands down."

Brody raised his brows. "You've convinced me. I don't normally like seafood, but will have to try some today."

Madison pointed into the distance. "Look, Lincoln just challenged Daniel to cornhole. He thinks that since he beat you that he can beat anyone now."

"The boy does have a good arm."

Madison smiled up at Brody. "I think he had a great time playing with you."

"He's a great kid."

Sheriff Carl and Pastor Ray approached them. Pastor Ray extended his hand. "Detective Philips. Sheriff Carl here has told me a lot about you. Glad to see you found a reason to join us here at church."

Brody glanced at Madison. "Madison's a good reason, but I think I'm going to start coming here for other reasons. Better reasons, like working on my relationship with God."

A grin broke across Pastor Ray's face. "That's great news."

Sheriff Carl slapped Brody's arm in male affection. "I knew you'd come around. Been praying for it since we met."

Sheriff Carl had really been praying for him? That was a first.

He glanced down at Madison and saw her eyes glowing as she looked up at him. She placed her hand on his arm.

"That is great news. The Christian path isn't always the easiest for the journey. In fact, sometimes it's harder. But it's deeper, more rewarding and richer."

Sheriff Carl extended his hand. "Welcome again. I just had to grab some of this food before heading back into work."

"Any updates?"

Sheriff Carl's face turned grim. "No, none yet. But he'll mess up. No one can commit the perfect crime. They only think they can."

Just as Sheriff Carl walked away, Brody's cell phone rang. Detective Blackston, he noted. He had to take it.

"It looks like we have another lead on the medicine missing from the hospital. There's a nurse who moonlights here on weekends and works for the school system during the year. And yes, the nurse is a male. I wondered if you wanted to meet me at the hospital while I question him."

Brody glanced at the crowd at the church. Madison was surrounded by people here who loved her and looked out for her. He didn't want to leave her, but if he had to, then this would be the most opportune time. Besides, maybe this was the break they'd been hoping for.

"I'll be right there."

When Madison looked up at him expectantly, he said, "There's a lead I need to follow up on. Can I talk you into staying here until I get back?"

"Sure thing."

"And save me some of that catfish."

She smiled. "Now that I can't promise."

"And if you need anything, call me. Okay?"

"I will."

Brody jogged toward his car. Maybe this would

be the lead that would help them close in on the Suicide Bandit.

The sheriff was right—the killer would screw up sometime, and Brody wanted to be there when he did.

EIGHTEEN

The wind slapped the tablecloth, sending it flying into Madison's face. She caught the flimsy plastic and balled it up. The hurricane was on its way. She could feel it in the air. Even nature seemed to know, she mused, noticing how the birds were feisty today, flying here and there.

Madison helped a group of church members clean up after the picnic while Lincoln and Kayla had gone to children's choir practice inside the sanctuary. As soon as choir practice was over, Madison hoped that Brody would be back. She had promised to stay here until he returned.

The thought of Brody made her smile and hum to herself as she threw away piles of paper plates and plasticware. Brody had realized his need for God. Her heart pounded with contentment every time she thought about it. There was no bigger decision he could make. Did this mean they could have a future together?

She looked across the green lawn of the church

and saw Kayla charging toward her, cell phone in hand. Immediately Madison's guard went up. She hurried toward Kayla. Lincoln? Had something happened to Lincoln?

"Kayla? What's wrong?"

"Madison, you need to go to the hospital." Kayla's voice sounded urgent and her eyes looked strained.

"What do you mean? What happened? Is Lincoln okay?"

"No, no. Sorry, Lincoln is fine." Kayla sucked in a breath. "It's Brody. Someone cut the brake line in his car. He's in the hospital now."

Panic squeezed Madison's throat. She remembered the last call she'd gotten like this. The urgent, "Come to the hospital now. Your husband has been in a car accident."

Images from that day flashed into her mind, taunting her, causing an uncontrollable ache to hammer her heart.

Now Brody. What had happened to him? Was he okay?

"Brody's going to be all right, Madison. I just thought someone should go out there and be with him. He would say he doesn't want that, but he shouldn't be alone. Besides, he'll need a ride home. I have a choir full of preschoolers or I'd go out there myself."

"I'll be right there. Can I borrow your car?"

"Of course. Lincoln and I can catch a ride with someone else. We're close enough to even walk if we have to."

Madison grabbed Kayla's outstretched keys and ran toward the parking lot. Her hands trembled as she started her car.

The day she'd been called to the hospital for Reid had been similar to today. Overcast, hot, seemingly normal. They'd had an afternoon thunderstorm. His car had hydroplaned on the way home from work and he'd hit a tree. When the EMTs had brought him to the hospital, Reid had been put into a medically induced coma. He'd remained in the coma for three days until he died.

Lincoln had only been a year old, barely able to walk. Before that fateful accident Madison and Reid had talked about all the dreams they had for their son. Taking him to Disney World, Reid coaching his T-ball team, teaching him to ride a bike. Suddenly those dreams didn't matter. Only keeping Reid alive did.

She often thought back to that last conversation she'd had with her husband. It had been so uneventful. It had just been an ordinary day. She'd kissed him goodbye for work, said she'd see him in time for dinner. She still remembered that she'd made roast beef and mashed potatoes that evening. It was one of Reid's favorite meals. In her rush to get to the hospital she'd forgotten to turn the oven off. The house had been filled with smoke when she had returned. She'd been lucky it hadn't burned down.

Today, Madison crouched over the steering wheel for the entire drive to the hospital. Tension wouldn't leave her body, even if Kayla had said Brody was okay. Finally the hospital appeared. She found a parking spot and hurried toward the entrance.

As soon as she stepped back inside, she felt like she'd been punched in the gut. The smells, the sounds, the sights. When she'd been attacked, the rescue squad had taken her to a different hospital, as the area had several. This was the very same hospital where Reid had been taken after his accident.

Reid—it had hurt so much when she'd lost him. She couldn't bear to think about going through that again. Loving someone was great. But losing them was such a raw wound, one that never completely healed. She blanched at the memories as she rushed toward the information desk.

"I'm here to see Brody Philips."

The nurse gave her instructions to his room. Madison knew by the beating of her heart that she'd allowed herself to open up too much for Brody already. She'd made herself vulnerable in ways she shouldn't have. She had to distance herself from him. Her heart ached to think about it, but that ache was nothing compared to the ache of losing someone and having to start life over—alone.

She knocked at Brody's door until she heard him say, "Come in." She hesitantly pushed open the heavy door in time to see him close his cell phone. He grinned when he saw Madison, but she hardly saw the smile. Instead, she soaked in the scratches across his face, his busted lip, his bandaged shoulder.

"You didn't have to come."

She wrapped her arms over her chest. "I know. I wanted to."

The nurse scurried out of the way and Madison stepped closer. "What happened? How are you?"

"Someone cut my brake line. I tried to exit the highway but couldn't stop. I ended up colliding with another car. We all walked away with some scrapes and bruises, but we're okay."

"I'm glad."

He reached his hand out. She stared at it a moment before taking it. He pulled her toward him. "What's wrong?"

"Nothing's wrong. I was just worried."

"I appreciate you worrying about me, but I'm fine." Brody leaned closer. "Hey." He nudged up her chin. "Come here." He pulled her toward him and wrapped his arms around her. The action should have felt comforting. But instead Madison kept having flashes from that day she came to see her husband in the hospital. He'd never left. They had so many unfinished conversations, unrealized dreams.

"You sure you're okay?"

She nodded and stepped away, wiping at her tears. "I'm fine."

"Why do I feel like you just put a huge wall up, then?"

Madison shrugged. Even if she didn't lose Brody to death, there was a good chance that she would lose him once the newness of their relationship wore off. Brody wasn't the type to commit. He'd said so himself. "I can't do this, Brody."

"Do what?"

"Us. I'm just..." How did she explain? She couldn't find the words. "I'm glad you're okay, Brody, but I have to go."

She fled before he could see anymore of her pain or try to change her mind.

Brody stared after Madison. What had just happened? One moment he'd been convinced that his relationship with Madison was the real thing and could go the distance. The next minute Madison was fleeing from the room like Brody himself was her attacker.

What had spooked her? Had she changed her

mind? Realized how mixed up he really was and decided he didn't deserve a chance? He punched the pillow behind him, trying to ignore the thud that came with each heartbeat. He hadn't realized how empty his life felt until he met Madison and Lincoln. Now they'd both just slipped away.

A knock sounded at the door. His heart sped as he wondered if Madison had returned. His hope faded when Sheriff Carl stuck his head through the doorway. "Knock, knock. Mind if I come in?"

Brody shrugged. "Not at all."

Sheriff Carl noted Brody's cuts and bruises a moment before frowning. "This wasn't an accident."

"No, someone cut my brake line. God must have had his angels watching out for me to be able to walk away from that accident with only a few scrapes."

"God's always watching out for us. He would have been watching out for you even if the results today had been different. We have to trust that He's with us in the good and the bad times." Sheriff Carl stopped beside the bed and heaved in a breath. "I'll need to take a report from you on what happened."

"Of course." Brody didn't care at the moment. All he wanted to do was to chase after Madison, to find out the reasoning behind her change of heart, to see if he could convince her otherwise.

"I thought I'd give you a ride back home."

"I'd love one."

Sheriff Carl paused, and Brody knew he wanted to say something. He braced himself for whatever that might be. "Ran into Madison leaving the hospital."

Brody tensed at the reminder, and he scowled. "Yeah, she came for a few minutes."

Sheriff Carl nodded in what appeared to be a nonchalant manner. Brody had a feeling he was trying to make this conversation appear casual when it was anything but. "You seem to be getting close to her lately."

"She's an incredible woman. I want to see whoever is doing this to her brought to justice."

"And that's it? This is just a matter of justice?"

Brody shrugged. "I thought maybe there could be more to the story than that, but after today, I guess there isn't."

Sheriff Carl nodded to the hospital room. "This is the hospital where Reid was brought."

"He was in…a car accident." Was that what this was about? His heart ached for Madison. Today must have been like one big, bad flashback.

"Yes, he was killed in an auto accident on the way home from work one day." Sheriff Carl shifted. "I'm not speaking for Madison. Maybe her reaction had nothing to do with Reid's death.

But I know there are places where your memories are brought back so vividly that you feel like you've been taken back in time. The place where your spouse died is likely one of them."

"I can only imagine. That must have been terrible."

"Beyond terrible. I was the one who called her to the hospital. I saw how her life was changed in the blink of an eye."

"We see that every day on our jobs, don't we? It's always hard, no matter how many times you see it."

"Brody, I think it could be a good thing if you don't spend any time with Madison for a while. Besides the fact that she needs space right now, I'm afraid that if the killer is targeting you next that Madison is only going to get swept up in the whole mess to an even greater extent. Maybe distance is the best thing for both of you now. I'll assign someone else to watch over her until this man is behind bars."

Brody nodded. He couldn't even argue about that point because the sheriff was right. If he really loved Madison, then he had to let her walk away.

But letting her walk away was the last thing he wanted to do.

NINETEEN

The next morning Madison stared numbly at the TV as twenty-four-hour news coverage of the possible hurricane filled the airwaves. She barely heard anything. All she could think about was Reid, that day when she'd received the news about his accident. They'd loved each other so much and when he was taken from her, her whole world felt as if it was crashing around her. Why would she ever want to put herself through that again? Besides, she should be content with life as it was. She had Lincoln and he lit up her life immensely. She had a career she loved, even though she did struggle a bit with her bills sometimes. But life was good...wasn't it?

The wind blew a smattering of debris against the house. She couldn't stay here tonight. The area along the bay where her house was located had a tendency to flood with major storms, and she didn't want to be stuck here with no electricity. Kayla had said they could stay with her.

Apparently she and Daniel had had a huge fight after the church picnic and had decided a relationship wouldn't work out, so it sounded as if Kayla wouldn't mind the company, anyway. A small knot of apprehension tightened in her stomach when she remembered how she'd sent home the deputy stationed outside her house. She knew his wife needed help battening down the hatches, so to speak, before the storm hit. He'd promised to meet her back at Kayla's house in an hour. Madison should be able to manage just fine for an hour...but the knot in her stomach didn't go away. Thinking about that decision now would do no good, however. Instead, she turned her thoughts back to the storm.

Should she remind Brody about the flooding tendency on their street? No, she was sure he'd figure it out on his own. There was no need to see him and stir up all of those crazy emotions again. Besides, he probably wouldn't want to speak with her again after how she'd handled herself yesterday. She could have at least given him a ride home, but when she'd realized she needed to put distance between herself and her handsome neighbor, she knew if she didn't do it then that she could change her mind. Changing her mind wasn't an option. She had to stay strong.

Lincoln bounced back into the living room with his backpack on. "I'm ready!"

Madison ran through a checklist with him to make sure he'd packed everything he was supposed to. When she was satisfied, she clicked off the TV and reached for her son's hand. "Let's get out of this house before the storm blows in, then."

Outside the breeze tugged at her, whipping her hair and clothes and bags in different directions. This was going to be some storm. What had the weatherman said? A category three? It could be downgraded before reaching land, though. She only hoped it didn't cause too much damage.

As pellets of rain began plopping around them, they raced to the SUV and climbed inside. The moisture from their clothes met with the stifling heat of the vehicle's interior and steamed the windows around them. Ominous thunder boomed in the not-so-far distance.

"Mom?"

Madison cranked the engine and blared the AC. "Yes, honey?"

"Is Mr. Brody going to be at Ms. Kayla's?"

Her heart felt a pang momentarily and she glanced back at her son as she pulled from the soggy driveway. "No, sweetheart. He's not going to be there."

Lincoln frowned. "Why not?"

"Because he's a smart man. He'll figure out that being on the water during a hurricane isn't wise and he'll find someone else to stay with." As they passed Brody's house, Madison noted that his truck wasn't there, anyway. He was probably already somewhere else, ready to camp out for the night.

"I like Mr. Brody."

Madison gripped the wheel as pine straw and leaves whipped under the vehicle and across the windshield. "He's a nice man, Lincoln. I'm glad you like him."

"Is that what Daddy was like?"

Madison sucked in a breath and she braked momentarily at the surprise of the question. "What do you mean?"

"I mean, did Daddy like to play baseball? And would he have given me big hugs every time he saw me? Do you think he would have taught me to draw my favorite cartoon characters, just like Mr. Brody? And would he have played video games with me where I could beat him every time?"

Madison held back the tears that now rimmed her eyes. Her throat burned with emotions she tried to suppress. "I'm sure he would have, Lincoln. He loved you very much. You were one of the best things that ever happened to him. He was so happy on the day you were born. He couldn't stop staring at you and saying how beautiful you were."

"Mommy?"

"Yes?" She braced herself for Lincoln's next question, unsure if her heart could take any more. Lincoln wanted a father in his life so badly. He wanted that affirmation, that love that only a father could give.

"I don't want Mr. Brody to stop playing with me."

Her last conversation with Brody filled her thoughts. He definitely wasn't going to be around as much anymore. Lincoln would get over it with time—at least that's what she hoped. "Brody has to work, Lincoln. His job keeps him busy. I'm sure he'll still play with you some. Maybe not as much as he's played with you last week, though."

"Why can't he be my new daddy?"

Madison blinked. "Your new daddy?"

"I like him, so why not?"

"It doesn't work that way, honey. It's a little more complicated." A lot more complicated, actually. If only life were as easy as four-year-olds thought.

Madison breathed a sigh of relief when her cell phone rang. She'd gone into town today and replaced the one the killer had taken. She didn't feel comfortable not having a phone with her at all times, especially considering everything that had happened. She looked at the number and saw that it was her reporter friend Mark. She hesitated a moment before answering.

"Hey, Mark. What is it?" She forced herself not to sound chummy, lest Mark think he was going to use her for one of his news stories.

"Madison." The noise in the phone made it sound as if wind hit his mouthpiece. "I'm covering a story down here at the docks. I could really use a photographer."

"Then ask the editor to send one out."

"I can't get ahold of him. He doesn't even know I'm doing this story. But the story is nothing without a picture."

She tapped her finger impatiently against the steering wheel. "What could be so important?"

"Madison, you've got to see it. The hurricane is rolling in and you can see the edge of the storm over the water. The boats are rocking back and forth in the waves so hard it looks like they could tip. The birds are all scattering." What sounded like another burst of wind shot through the phone. "It's incredible. Just your speed. I know you love nature and all of that junk."

It did sound intriguing. But could Mark be trusted? What if he was the one behind these attacks? She had to be careful. She also had to live her life without grasping on to the fear that those who lived without Christ seemed to embrace. "I appreciate you thinking of me. I'll think about it."

"Look, Madison, it will only take a few minutes of your time. And you won't even have to come near me. I know you had me investigated… but I'm not the killer. I feel bad about cornering you earlier. I want to make it up to you and give you this great photo. I think it will get you noticed." The phone line crackled. Was Mark telling the truth?

Before she could say anything else, the line went dead. Must be because of the storm moving in.

She tucked her phone back into her purse. Several minutes later she pulled up to Kayla's place. The rain had stopped again amidst the churning clouds. She helped Lincoln from the SUV and made a run for Kayla's front porch. Madison was surprised to see Daniel pull up at the same time. Young love. It could be like a soap opera sometimes, Madison mused.

Madison paused on the porch and pulled her hair out of her face. Kayla grinned broadly from the doorway. "Kayla, I don't want to impose on you. I know I've already done that enough. But I need to go take a quick picture. Could Lincoln stay here just a few minutes until I get back?"

Kayla looked at the darkening sky. "Are you sure it's safe to go out there?"

"I'm just headed to the docks for a moment. I want to take a snapshot for the newspaper."

"If you think you'll be okay. Of course Lincoln can stay here."

"How about if I ride with you?" Daniel asked, stepping out of his car. "You can never be too safe in times like these."

Did he mean with the storm or with the serial killer on the loose? Either way his point was a good one. Besides, he was strong and athletic and, if Mark was behind the recent attacks, then Madison would feel safer if Daniel were along.

"I'd appreciate that, Daniel. You're right—you can never be too safe."

He kissed Kayla's cheek, and she grinned up at him. "I'll see you in a few."

They hurried to the SUV and climbed inside. Madison resisted the urge to ask what was going on between him and Kayla. Kayla would tell Madison in time, she supposed. Besides, she didn't know Daniel well enough to ask a question like that.

"You ever been through a hurricane before, Daniel?"

"No, not really. I'm from up north originally. We get nor'easters mostly. But I never lived on the coast. I hear flooding can be bad here."

"I never knew you were from up north. How long have you been here again?"

"Almost eight months. Seaford's a great place. I love it."

"I like it, too. Good place to raise a family." She glanced over at him. "Rumor has it that you played for a baseball farm team before coming here. That true?"

"I was actually a gymnast."

"A gymnast? Wow. I would never have guessed."

"I had an injury and had to stop competing. I went into sports medicine, instead."

"And now you're a teacher? I'd say you're pretty well-rounded with all of those careers under your belt." She pulled up to the docks, her gaze grazing the area. There was a banquet hall, a bait and tackle shop and a small marina that all shared a beat-up parking lot. She didn't see Mark anywhere, but any of the boats in the distance could obscure her view of him.

She put the SUV in park, strung her camera around her neck, and stepped outside for a better look. She grabbed her hair and raked it back from her face as the wind beat against her. She appeared too late for the picture that Mark had promised her. The clouds in the distance still looked ominous, but not exactly photogenic.

Daniel appeared beside her, following her gaze. "See him?"

"No, I assumed he'd be in the parking lot. I'm not really fond of searching for him with this storm coming."

"I'd feel the same way." Daniel turned toward

her and tilted his head. "Did I ever tell you that you look just like someone I used to know, Madison?"

Madison turned toward him, still clipping her hair back with her fingers. "Do I? Who's that?"

"My sister."

She smiled. "I always wanted a sister or brother. You're lucky to have one."

"She passed away last year, actually."

"I'm sorry to hear that. That must have been terribly hard."

"Beyond words."

Her heart beat with compassion. "I know all about that kind of grief."

"Because you lost your husband?"

"Yes. There are no words to describe how much that hurts." *And remember, you never want to go through that again, even if Lincoln is totally taken by Brody.*

"I knew there was something special about you the first time I saw you, Madison."

Her compassion turned to unease. She swallowed, but the lump in her throat remained. "There's nothing special about me. I'm just a single mom and a photographer. Pretty boring by most standards." She stepped away. "I really need to find Mark and let him know I got here too late for a photo." She glanced around, but saw no sign of him. "Better yet, maybe I'll just take this picture and get back to Kayla's. The sky looks like it's going to burst any time now."

"Good idea."

She held up her camera and snapped her first picture. Daniel's odd actions wouldn't leave her mind though, and she was painfully aware of his presence. She wanted to run, to escape. But Daniel could easily catch her. Instead, she'd try to play it safe, to act like his words hadn't strung her nerves like a tightrope.

Did the man simply have an odd crush on her? Or was there more to it than that?

Based on the level of fear she felt at the moment, she thought she had her answer.

Brody tried to immerse himself in his work at the station. At least that way he'd forget about Madison and the fact that he had zero chance with her. How could he ask her to risk so much again? He knew the answer. He couldn't.

As the wind beat down on the building, even caused the lights to flicker, he opened the file on Lindsey's death. He'd called one of the detectives in New York and had the files sent down to him. Brody had the strange feeling that the cases were connected somehow, and he hoped that something in these reports might trigger a realization in him.

He flipped through the pages, reliving the horrors of finding her, of realizing that it was his fault that she'd taken her life.

God could wash away all of your sins. He reminded himself of that fact. He had to believe it, had to have faith that forgiveness was possible, just like he and Madison had talked about, just like the pastor had spoken of on Sunday.

He closed his eyes and prayed for God's help in letting go of the hurts he held on to.

And, Jesus, I know I need You in my life. I'm tired of living for myself, and I know there's more to life than my own happiness.

God had already begun changing his heart, he felt sure. And he felt confident that God would keep on working on him.

When he opened his eyes, he felt lighter.

With renewed energy Brody looked at the police report before him. He soaked in all of the details surrounding Lindsey's suicide. There'd even been that note she'd left. Someone had killed her and made it look like a suicide.

He seemed to remember someone in Lindsey's family had suspected it to be murder the entire time. Who was that? He remembered: her brother. What were those reasons he'd given again? He did a quick search on his computer and easily found her brother's name. Then he picked up the phone and gave him a call.

A woman answered. Brody explained who he was and asked to speak with Richard.

"This is Richard's old girlfriend. He moved out about nine months ago and left me with a stack full of bills and a whole lot of heartache."

"Do you know where he went?"

"Virginia. Said he took a teaching job at a high school there. If you find him, can you tell him he owes me two thousand dollars?"

Brody froze a moment. Virginia? High-school teacher?

Daniel. Could it be?

Brody imagined the baseball coach a little younger with longer hair, tan skin and twenty pounds heavier. Clearly, he remembered what Lindsey's brother looked like. He looked like Daniel. He *was* Daniel.

He dropped the phone and started toward the door. He had to find Kayla and Madison. Neither of them was safe.

How did she get away from Daniel without clueing him in that she was frightened? And where was Mark?

From where Madison stood, her SUV was farther away than the bait and tackle shop at the water's edge. Plus, Daniel stood between her and the SUV. But maybe she could make it to the shop.

Maybe the business was still open. There was still a car out in front of it.

She squinted. Was that Mark's car? Was he inside waiting for her? Some of the locals were crazy and insisted staying at the bayside homes and businesses when storms like this one came in. Perhaps someone who could help was inside. What other options did she have at the moment?

"I'm going to check and see if Mark is inside," she told Daniel. When she glanced up at him, something looked different about his face. His eyes almost looked glazed and too still for the moment—like glassy water that had currents rippling underneath, just out of sight.

"Good idea."

"I'll be right back!" She called as she hurried away. She prayed he would stay there and not follow her. All of her guards were on full alert. Something was up with Daniel, and she feared it was more than a failed romantic attempt.

She grabbed the door handle and jerked it. The motion, along with a gust of wind, caused the door to fly open and slap against the building. Her heart beat in double time. She glanced back once more and saw Daniel standing in the parking lot, his hands in his pockets, staring at her blankly. Shivers raced up her spine.

She reached into her pocket and grabbed her phone. She had to call Brody. Before she dialed the number, something in the background grabbed her attention. Was that…

"Mark?" She stepped closer and gasped. Mark sat on a stool, a gag over his mouth and a rope around his neck. He stared at her, his eyes wide, pleading…terrified. "What…?"

She had to call Brody. Now. Her fingers fumbled over the numbers, her hands shaking so badly that she could barely find the correct keys.

"That's not a good idea, Madison."

She gasped and twirled around. Daniel. The still, quiet look in his eyes had been replaced with some kind of spark, a mischievous glint, that only intensified her tremors. She backed up, toward Mark. She hadn't gotten to the last digit of Brody's phone number yet. If she could simply find it, feel her way around the keypad without Daniel noticing…

"Give me the phone, Madison." Daniel reached out his hand, like a teacher might do to a student holding something illegal.

"Daniel, I need to call for help. My friend is hurt. He needs help." She tried to keep her voice steady, consistent.

He stepped toward her and at once Madison realized how tall he stood, how strong the muscles were under his T-shirt. "You're not calling anyone, Madison. Don't play dumb. You know who I am."

"Who are you, Daniel?"

He smiled. "I'm the Suicide Bandit. And I'm sorry to say, but your time is up."

TWENTY

Brody gripped his cell phone as he barreled down the road. Finally Kayla answered her cellular. He could hear Lincoln playing in the background and his heartbeat slowed some. Maybe Madison and Kayla were both safe, and he'd reached them in time. "Kayla, where are you?"

"I'm at home waiting for the storm to hit. Why?"

Good, his cousin was okay for now. But she was only part of his concern. "Where's Madison? Have you talked to her lately? Is she there?"

"Madison? She went to take a picture for the newspaper, but she should be back in a few minutes. She dropped off Lincoln."

The wind swept under his car as he drove and rocked it back and forth. He continued charging ahead. "Listen to me very carefully, Kayla. If Daniel shows up at your door, I need you to pretend you're not home. Do whatever you need, but stay away from him. Do you understand?"

"Stay away from Daniel? Why? Why would you say that?" Her voice rose in pitch, in confusion.

There was no gentle way to break the news to Kayla that the man she'd been dating was a killer. With no time to waste, he threw niceties aside. "He's the Suicide Bandit, Kayla."

"No..." Her voice trailed off in disbelief. "Brody, that can't be true. He can't be..."

"I'll explain everything when I have the chance. Just promise me you'll stay away from him, Kayla."

"I promise. But Brody..."

Something about the way she said those words made his muscles tighten. "What is it, Kayla?"

"Daniel's with Madison. He offered to go with her in case there were any problems with the storm."

Fear pulsed through Brody, and he pressed the accelerator even harder. "Where'd they go?"

"To the docks."

Brody hung up and raced toward the water. He just prayed he wasn't too late.

"Why would you want to kill anyone, Daniel? You're a nice guy. That doesn't make any sense." Madison backed closer to Mark and farther away from Daniel.

"I'm not all that nice, Madison." Daniel pulled

out a syringe, popped the top off and pushed all the air out before grinning. "You know your boyfriend left a killer on the streets? He was arrogant enough to think that my sister took her own life after he'd broken her heart. Brody wouldn't listen to me. I tried to tell him that it was murder disguised as suicide, but to those NYC detectives the case was open-and-shut."

"Maybe they'll listen now."

Daniel grinned again. "That's what I'm hoping. It's a shame that I had to take things to this extreme to get their attention, however."

Madison stared at the needle, her imagination already feeling its prick and the oozy aftereffects. But this time Daniel might not simply knock her out. Whatever was in that syringe could kill her.

"So this has all been about Brody?" *Keep him talking, Madison. Keep him talking.*

"I needed to get his attention. That's why I targeted his pretty neighbor. But then you survived and I realized the poor guy was simply enamored with you." He shrugged. "That's when you became my pawn in this game. He hurt the person I loved most, so now I'll hurt the person he loves the most."

"He doesn't love me, Daniel."

"Don't be ridiculous. Of course he does. It's written all over his face. You're different from his other girlfriends. You're more like my sister.

You're beautiful, but grounded. You have more to offer than just a good time."

"You're right. She does have a lot to offer, and I love her."

Madison gasped at the deep voice booming from the doorway. Brody. He'd found her. Her relief was only momentary.

Brody slowly stepped inside, his hands raised in surrender. "I'm the one you're angry with, Daniel. Why don't you let them go and take this up with me?"

"Because that would make you appear noble. That's not what I want." Daniel clicked his tongue as he shook his head. He pulled a gun from his waistband. "Not what I want at all." He aimed his weapon at Brody.

Madison's heart flinched in fear. *Don't shoot Brody. Don't shoot Brody. I need to tell him how much I care about him.*

And she did care about him. No matter how much she tried to deny her feelings, she cared. It didn't matter if they were in a relationship or not—at this point, losing him would hurt either way.

Now she just needed to tell Brody that she was willing to risk her heart again.

Faith not fear.

She breathed in a prayer. She needed to have faith that God would provide the out they needed, that He would protect them. Fear would only paralyze her right now.

Wind rocked the entire store as the storm got closer. If Daniel didn't kill them all, then the hurricane might. The building swayed under the strength of the beast. One big gust could send them all into the bay and scrambling for their lives.

With the gun pointed at Brody and the needle at her, Daniel smirked. "Madison, untie your friend over there." Daniel pointed at Mark.

She hurried toward him and fumbled with the tie at his wrists. Finally his hands released from their binds. Mark quickly scrambled to get the noose off and to jerk down the gag at his mouth.

Daniel nodded toward the door. "Leave. You were just the bait to get them here."

Mark's eyes darted from Madison to Brody, and sweat poured down his face. After what appeared to be a moment of contemplation, he ran from the building without looking back.

Daniel looked at the chair before nodding to Madison. "Sit."

Madison tried to swallow, but her mouth was too dry. What was this leading up to? Her entire body trembled as she obeyed Daniel's instructions.

"Brody, tie up your little girlfriend. I'm going to teach you both a lesson now."

Brody stepped forward, his gaze on Madison, as if trying to reassure her that everything would be okay. As he stepped behind her, Daniel hovered closer.

"Amazing what you can get online, isn't it? No, this isn't the other stuff I injected you with. This—" he squirted a drop from the tip of the needle "—is enough codeine to take you from this life for good. Or at least leave you in a vegetative state."

Brody's hand rested on her shoulder. "You don't want to do that, Daniel. Please, just let her go."

Daniel took a step closer, the needle in his hands poised for injection. Madison shuddered at his nearness. Codeine. He'd said he used to work in sports medicine. No wonder he had syringes and knowledge about the medicines.

Madison shifted, trying to buy time as she searched for an escape route. "How'd you get into all of those houses, Daniel? It was almost like you were a ghost. No signs of forced entry."

He smiled, the vacant expression making her shudder. "Easy. I was friends with all of you. I simply swiped the keys out, made copies and returned them before anyone noticed. Simple."

What did they have to fight back with? There had to be something...

An idea hit her. Her camera. It was dark enough

that their eyes would be blinded by the shock of the camera flash. If Madison could throw him off balance for a second, perhaps Brody could tackle him.

Of course this was all dependant on both her flash working correctly and Brody somehow reading her mind.

Lord, help us.

The wind rocked the building again. Something creaked outside. Madison feared the sound came from the building's frame. Rain pounded at the roof. Waves, once lapping, now angrily smashed the underside of the store.

The sudden cry of the storm even seemed to distract Daniel for a moment. Seizing the opportunity, Madison raised her camera and began repeatedly snapping the flash.

Daniel blinked and backed up a step. Brody didn't miss a beat. He lunged forward and knocked the gun from his hands.

The building groaned again and visibly shifted.

Madison grabbed the shelf beside her to gain steadiness, but all the tackle supplies crashed to the floor.

Daniel and Brody slammed into the opposite wall. Daniel still held the syringe. Brody grabbed his hands and fought him back. Daniel's hands curled as he tried to direct the needle toward Brody.

Madison's gaze swept the place until she found a fire extinguisher. She slammed it into Daniel's head. He sank to the ground just as the building rocked again.

"Come on," Brody said. "We've got to get out of here." He grabbed her hand and they fought their way upward as water began pouring into the building. The bay and the hurricane tried to eat away at the building with them still inside. The waves had begun to separate the framework, to break away the siding.

Madison slipped and started sliding with the building toward the water. Brody jerked her arm, holding her. In one motion he propelled her out the entrance. She held on to him, her muscles straining, as the building fell into the bay. Daniel was swept out to sea with it.

Brody pulled himself onto the concrete slab that had once been a sidewalk. Rain pounded at them, the wind visibly swayed them. At the moment it didn't matter.

Brody cupped Madison's face with his hands and planted a kiss on her lips before wrapping her in a bear hug.

They'd survived. Barely, but that was enough for Madison.

Shortly after the hurricane had washed the bait and tackle shop into the bay, Sheriff Carl had arrived at the docks to pick up Madison and Brody—Mark had at least been courteous enough to call the cops after he'd fled. Sheriff Carl had taken their statements, and the paramedics had examined them for injuries.

As soon as the storm had cleared, divers went in search of Daniel's body. To Madison's relief, they'd found it floating a few miles away. They discovered that Daniel had been taking steroids, which only added to his psychotic behavior.

Brody had called his former colleagues in New York City and they'd promised to look into Lindsey's case again. Kayla had cried over her realizations about Daniel. Lincoln had crawled all over Brody, apparently thankful to have him close by again.

Through all of that, Madison hadn't had a moment alone with Brody yet. Though they'd stolen glances and offered each other hugs and support, they hadn't talked about anything yet. She was getting anxious.

That moment finally came after Madison put Lincoln to bed. Two days had passed since they'd found Daniel's body and life had returned to their new—and safe—normal. Kayla, Sheriff Carl and Bonnie had come over for a cookout, and everyone had hung out talking and playing games in the backyard long after the sun set. The day received Madison's stamp of approval. But now she was anxious to talk to Brody, to have a moment alone with him.

She rubbed her hands on her jeans as she sat next to Brody on the couch. "I thought that boy was never going to fall asleep."

Brody grinned and slipped his arm around her shoulders, pulling her close. "I hope I didn't keep him up too late playing catch. The boy's got a good arm. He'll definitely be ready for T-ball next year."

Madison smiled. The way Brody talked about T-ball made it sound like he might still be around next year to help out. "He loved playing ball with you. And even though he was up past his bedtime, I don't care. He deserves a break after everything that's happened."

Madison pulled away from Brody for a moment so she could look in his eyes. "Brody…"

"What's wrong, Madison?"

She shook her head. "Nothing's wrong. I just…I just wanted to talk about everything that's happened, about what's going on between us."

Brody's eyes warmed and he grasped her hand. "I'm glad you asked because I've been wanting a moment with you to myself so I could bring that very subject up." He angled himself toward her and drew in a breath. "I've never met anyone like you before, Madison. I can't imagine what my future would be like without you—and Lincoln—at my side. I was hoping you might feel the same way."

She sighed, pleasure filling her heart. She gripped his hand tighter. "Brody, everything that's happened has reminded me that we're not promised tomorrow. I have to stop fearing that realization and start making the most of each moment, instead. I want to risk again, Brody. I can't imagine my tomorrows without you by my side, either."

Brody grinned. "I love you, Madison."

"Even though the journey to bring us to this point has been crazy, I'm so glad we're where we are." She tenderly cupped his face. "I love you, too, Brody Philips."

EPILOGUE

Eight months later

April in Seaford was beautiful. The trees and foliage gently morphed from brown to green. The birds returned to the area, squawking their God-given songs. The breeze from the bay began to bring warmth instead of chills.

This Saturday in April was no different. The sky shone bright and blue. The temperature felt mild and inviting. Life seemed full of possibilities.

Madison smiled as Brody reached over and clutched her hand as they stood at the end of the pier outside her home. Brody had helped enlarge the space, adding a deck at the end complete with railing where they could lounge on lazy, warm days. Ten people could easily fit into the space now.

And they did.

"Madison?"

Madison squeezed the flowers in her hands as she turned to Brody, who stared down at her with eyes full of warmth. "Yes?"

"I love you."

A grin broke across her face, an occurrence that had been happening a lot over the past several months. "I love you, too, Brody Philips."

"Are you ever going to pronounce them husband and wife, Pastor Dan?" Sheriff Carl asked from the plastic chair a few feet away.

Pastor Ray smiled. "Hold your horses, Carl. I'm getting to it."

"I'm going to have to turn on my sirens in order to get you to hurry things along here." Sheriff Carl shook his head, still grinning.

"Oh, Carl," Bonnie elbowed him. "Leave them alone and stop interrupting things."

Madison laughed, grateful to be surrounded by the people closest to her today. Her parents had flown up from Florida. Brody's dad had come down from Pennsylvania. Kayla had come, of course, with a new beau at her side. Everyone was here who needed to be here.

Pastor Ray cleared his throat. "Marriage is a serious commitment. I have a poem here—"

"Pastor Ray, no offense, but could you move it along a bit?" Brody said.

"Getting cold feet?" Madison asked, watching

as her fiancé's expression sparkled with a touch of mischief.

"Never. I'm just ready for you to become Mrs. Brody Philips."

With an expression of suppressed humor, Pastor Ray threw his small black notebook behind him. "Okay, forget all of the beautiful things I had planned to say about marriage. Brody, do you take this woman to be your wife?"

"I do."

"Madison, do you take this man to be your husband?"

"I do."

"Lincoln, do you support Brody becoming your father?"

"Yes!" Lincoln said with enough excitement to send chuckles through the crowd.

"In that case and, without further ado, I pronounce you man and wife. You may kiss the bride."

Brody stepped forward and his lips met Madison's. As Lincoln made a noise to show his disgust, Madison and Brody pulled away with a chuckle. Brody pulled her into a warm hug, their foreheads touching.

Brody's eyes seemed to glimmer as he looked down at her. "Eight months and no regrets. I feel lucky each day to have you in my life."

Madison couldn't resist another grin. "I'd say God's blessed both of us."

Lincoln tugged on her white dress. "Mom?"

Madison rubbed her son's already tousled hair. "I'm sorry—I mean God's blessed all three of us."

And he certainly had, Madison thought. She'd found happiness again and her family was complete. What more could she ask for? She smiled at Brody and Lincoln. Nothing, she decided. Absolutely nothing.

* * * * *

Dear Reader,

I live close to both the Chesapeake Bay and the ocean. There's just something about sitting on the shore and watching the waves roll in that calms my soul. One of my favorite beaches is on the Chesapeake Bay. The water is gentler there and the shores less crowded. I have a favorite spot there that happens to be nestled beside a military base. Oftentimes you can work on your tan all while watching Special Operations perform training exercises on the shore. You can find horseshoe crabs and shells. You can listen to children laughing and fishermen shooting the breeze. And there on the shores, stories are born. Characters come to life. In this I'm reminded of God's creativity and His love for me. If there's something in your life that you need to forgive yourself for, remember how much God loves his creatures—especially you.

Christy Barritt

Questions for Discussion

1. Brody acknowledges that in his past, he didn't give enough thought to how he treated people. He regrets that today. How do you treat people? Any regrets?

2. Brody feels guilt over his past. Is there anything you still feel guilty about? What actions can you take to relieve that guilt?

3. Is guilt always caused by sin or is it sometimes caused by the enemy, as well? Are there times when our guilt isn't justified? How can you know the difference?

4. Sometimes the hardest person to forgive is ourselves. What are some simple steps we can take to make this happen?

5. Why is forgiving ourselves important? If we don't forgive ourselves, how does that effect us emotionally, spiritually and even physically?

6. Read Matthew 6:15. Even more than forgiving ourselves, we desperately need God's forgiveness in our lives. How can we obtain that?

7. Madison and her husband dreamed dreams together that were unrealized after his death. What's the hardest part of realizing your dreams are out of reach? How can we find hope in knowing that God can change our dreams into something even more beautiful when we trust Him?

8. Madison has already lost one man that she loved. She fears losing someone else in her life and the pain that inevitably comes with that. How can we rise above our fears? Why is this important?

9. Read Philippians 4:6. Fear and anxiety often go hand in hand. How does the Bible say to get rid of anxiety?

10. If we never did anything we feared, we'd be stuck in a self-made comfort zone. Growth happens when we aren't afraid to risk. Is there a fear you need to conquer in order that you might grow stronger?

LARGER-PRINT BOOKS!

**GET 2 FREE
LARGER-PRINT NOVELS
PLUS 2 FREE
MYSTERY GIFTS**

Love Inspired®
SUSPENSE
RIVETING INSPIRATIONAL ROMANCE

Larger-print novels are now available...

YES! Please send me 2 FREE LARGER-PRINT Love Inspired® Suspense novels and my 2 FREE mystery gifts (gifts are worth about $10). After receiving them, if I don't wish to receive any more books, I can return the shipping statement marked "cancel". If I don't cancel, I will receive 4 brand-new novels every month and be billed just $4.99 per book in the U.S. or $5.49 per book in Canada. That's a saving of at least 23% off the cover price. It's quite a bargain! Shipping and handling is just 50¢ per book in the U.S. and 75¢ per book in Canada.* I understand that accepting the 2 free books and gifts places me under no obligation to buy anything. I can always return a shipment and cancel at any time. Even if I never buy another book, the two free books and gifts are mine to keep forever.

110/310 IDN FEH3

Name	(PLEASE PRINT)

Address	Apt. #

City	State/Prov.	Zip/Postal Code

Signature (if under 18, a parent or guardian must sign)

Mail to the **Reader Service:**
IN U.S.A.: P.O. Box 1867, Buffalo, NY 14240-1867
IN CANADA: P.O. Box 609, Fort Erie, Ontario L2A 5X3

Not valid for current subscribers to Love Inspired Suspense larger-print books.

**Are you a current subscriber to Love Inspired Suspense books
and want to receive the larger-print edition?
Call 1-800-873-8635 or visit www.ReaderService.com.**

* Terms and prices subject to change without notice. Prices do not include applicable taxes. Sales tax applicable in N.Y. Canadian residents will be charged applicable taxes. Offer not valid in Quebec. This offer is limited to one order per household. All orders subject to credit approval. Credit or debit balances in a customer's account(s) may be offset by any other outstanding balance owed by or to the customer. Please allow 4 to 6 weeks for delivery. Offer available while quantities last.

Your Privacy—The Reader Service is committed to protecting your privacy. Our Privacy Policy is available online at www.ReaderService.com or upon request from the Reader Service.

We make a portion of our mailing list available to reputable third parties that offer products we believe may interest you. If you prefer that we not exchange your name with third parties, or if you wish to clarify or modify your communication preferences, please visit us at www.ReaderService.com/consumerschoice or write to us at Reader Service Preference Service, P.O. Box 9062, Buffalo, NY 14269. Include your complete name and address.